# THE FIDDLER'S WALTZ

In post-war Liverpool, Ellen Butterworth's ambitious sweetheart Brian leaves the Navy and comes ashore so they can begin a future together. An urgent telegram from her younger sister Jeanette interrupts their wedding plans, and Ellen must return to the Yorkshire wool town where she grew up. Unexpectedly, Brian follows her — he wants them to be married there and then in Yorkshire! But, from the moment Jeanette appears in the room, Brian isn't able to take his eyes off her . . .

JUNE DAVIES

# THE
# FIDDLER'S
# WALTZ

*Complete and Unabridged*

## LINFORD
*Leicester*

First published in Great Britain in 2010

First Linford Edition
published 2015

A catalogue record for this book is available
from the British Library.

ISBN 978–1–4448–2622–7

Published by
F. A. Thorpe (Publishing)
Anstey, Leicestershire

Set by Words & Graphics Ltd.
Anstey, Leicestershire
Printed and bound in Great Britain by
T. J. International Ltd., Padstow, Cornwall

This book is printed on acid-free paper

# 1

The estuary was busy this morning, Ellen noticed absently, glancing from the window down over the rooftops to the slate-grey waters of the Mersey. Workmanlike vessels from all points of the compass were sailing in with the tide, while nippy little tugs skimmed out across ragged, foam-crested waves to guide the laden ships through the hazardous sandbars safely into port.

Ellen sighed, holding her last pair of nylons up to the daylight and grimacing at the tiny ladder appearing in one of the heels. Hopefully, a dab of clear nail varnish would stop it running up the entire leg.

'Do you fancy going to the pictures tonight, Hilary?' She turned to her roommate. 'Betty Grable's on at the Royalty. We could splash out and go to Sweetings for tea and cakes — it *is* pay-day, after all!'

'Sounds good.' Hilary replied, not looking around from the dressing-table mirror as she slid the final grip into her hair, anchoring it into its rather severe style. 'I don't mean to pry, Nell, but don't you think you should be asking Brian to go with you? It's ages since the pair of you had a night out.'

'Don't I know it!' responded Ellen, pushing her feet into stout high heels. 'When he got out of the Navy, I thought we'd be together all the while, but it seems like we're seeing less and less of each other as the weeks go by!'

'Brian must've been very young when he was called up during the war,' commented the older woman sympathetically. 'After years at sea, he's bound to find civilian life difficult.'

'I understand that. Really, I do,' went on Ellen bleakly. 'But he's been ashore months now! Days go by when we don't even *see* each other and he never wants to go out anywhere — unless it's on his own to play billiards at the

Seamen's Mission they've set up in that bombed-out church. He won't even come round for Sunday dinner any more, although I've asked him often.'

'Perhaps Mrs Cummings has scared him off!' suggested Hilary lightly, although her eyes were concerned for her friend. Neither woman was from Liverpool. They'd met during the war, working side by side making barrage balloons, and struck up a friendship that had extended beyond the factory gates and continued after peace was finally declared. 'Our landlady has a heart of gold, but she can be rather fierce with gentleman callers!'

Ellen shook her head. 'Brian can charm the birds from the trees. Mrs Cummings thinks the world of him. And whenever he was on leave, he'd always come around doing odd jobs about the house and tidying the garden for her. No, it isn't that,' she finished, taking her coat from the cupboard. 'Brian and I used to be really close, but I don't know where I am with him any more.'

3

Hilary's gaze slid to the framed wedding photograph on her dressing-table.

'After we married, Bernard came home on leave just once. He was a different person, Nell. I didn't know what to say, or how to talk to him. It was almost as though we needed to get to know each other all over again.'

Ellen paused. That period of leave from the RAF was the last time Hilary saw her husband. Bernard was shot down and captured. He'd perished early in 1945, during the long march from a prisoner-of-war camp in Poland.

'This is different, Hil. Brian chose to stay in the Navy after the war ended. When we met and fell in love, he came ashore so we could be together — but he's just been drifting from job to job and nothing's going right!'

'He's been at Hathersedge's over a month, which is far longer than he held down any of the other jobs,' ventured Hilary optimistically. 'Surely that's a sign Brian's starting to settle down?'

'You're right,' considered Ellen thoughtfully. 'Brian wasn't keen on becoming second assistant in gents' outfitting at Hathersedge's, but he has buckled down and done his best to fit in.'

'No easy task, swapping a life on the ocean wave for the third floor of a department store!' Hilary smiled, taking up her handbag and gloves and starting out onto the landing. 'We must tell Mrs Cummings we won't be in for tea. Shall we meet outside Sweetings?'

'Perfect!' Ellen hurried down the stairs, jamming her hat firmly onto her flyaway chestnut curls. 'I'll get the tram from Hathersedge's in plenty of time for tea and cakes before the big picture — I *do* love Fridays!'

★　★　★

'Thank you, Miss Butterworth,' said Mark Hathersedge later that morning, adding his signature to the last of the freshly-typed letters and handing the sheaf of crisp pages back to her. 'And be sure my father and brothers receive full copies of the Turkish emporium correspondence before the end of business today. It's vital we are in complete agreement before committing ourselves to contract.'

'I'll see to it straight away, sir.'

'I was speaking to Mr Poppleton earlier,' he remarked. 'Although he was naturally reluctant to take somebody without experience into his department — but did so out of deference to your recommendation — Mr Poppleton informs me your Mr Kennedy is proving quite satisfactory as second assistant.

'I recall your anxiety when you enquired as to whether your young man might be considered for the vacancy in gents' outfitting, and thought you would be heartened to learn the appointment appears to be progressing well.'

'Yes. Oh, yes! I am, sir!' exclaimed Ellen, relieved and overjoyed. 'Brian doesn't talk much about his work — about anything, really — I'm so glad

Mr Poppleton is pleased with him!'

Hathersedge inclined his head slightly. 'Gerard Poppleton has a reputation as a martinet, Miss Butterworth. He came to Hathersedge's more than thirty years ago, after he was invalided out of the army during the Great War. I suspect Gerard understands the difficulties former servicemen face and has made allowances accordingly.'

Ellen slipped from his office and closed the door behind her. She felt like dancing around her own little office! Now Brian was settled in a steady job, the worst was surely over and they could finally begin to make plans for their future!

She'd no sooner popped the letters into envelopes ready for the next post when the telephone rang.

'Good morning, Mark Hathersedge's office — oh, hello, Bill! Yes, yes. That's right. He's a linen manufacturer from Burnley. Come for a meeting with Mr Mark. I'll be right down to greet him. Oh, and Bill, they're going for lunch at the Excelsior Hotel, so can you please have the car brought round at twelve-thirty?'

With a polite tap upon the oak door, Ellen popped her head into Mark Hathersedge's office. 'Mr Abbott's arrived, sir!'

'Everything's arranged for luncheon, isn't it?' he queried, glancing up. 'When we leave for the Excelsior, take your lunch break straight away so you'll be back at your desk before I return.'

'Yes, sir.' She stepped forward. 'Here are the fabric swatches you asked for.'

'Good, good.' He flipped through the clip of samples. 'Off you go and fetch him up — and will you sort out a tray of tea and biscuits before you come in with your notepad?'

'Kettle's already on, sir,' replied Ellen, disappearing around the door and sprinting down the marble staircase to welcome their visitor.

★ ★ ★

The instant the two businessmen left for their luncheon at the Excelsior Hotel, Ellen hurriedly stowed her shorthand pad and pencil in her desk drawer, took out her handbag and started briskly down to the staff canteen.

The first sitting had been and gone, the second and third not yet come, so the huge room with its rows of oblong tables was almost deserted. Smiling hello to Beryl, the canteen's manager, Ellen was making her way towards the counter when, from the corner of her eye, she spotted Brian tucked away at the back of the room. His lunchtime wasn't for another hour! Ellen felt a wave of apprehension.

Turning from the counter, she hurried the length of the empty canteen. Although her heels sounded loud on the pale green linoleum, Brian didn't seem aware of her approach. A cup of tea, half-eaten meal and open newspaper were spread across the table before him, but he'd pushed them aside and was lounging comfortably back in his chair. Slowly drawing on a cigarette, he was engrossed in reading a hand-written letter. The envelope, with its brightly-coloured foreign stamps, lay discarded next to his teacup.

When finally he did glance up from the pages, surprise lit his brown eyes and the familiar, lazy smile that never failed to make Ellen's heart beat faster spread across the strong, tanned face.

'Hello, queen! Fancy seeing you here! On your lunch already?'

'Erm, yes.' She stared at him. The top button of his shirt was unfastened and his tie casually loosened — that alone would bring censure from the manage-ment, for slovenly appearance was not tolerated, even here in the canteen. 'Mr Mark told me to take an early lunch.'

'If the great man told you to, that explains it!' grinned Brian, pushing the letter into its envelope and rising from the table. 'What are you eating? Beryl tells me the bacon fritters are the dish least likely to cause food poisoning.'

'Beryl told you no such thing, and

the food here is extremely wholesome,' remarked Ellen distractedly, taking a seat. 'I don't want anything, not yet anyway. Brian, whatever are you doing here at this hour?'

'Kismet, queen. Fate conspired to have me sitting here with my gasper at the very moment Mr Mark told you to take an early lunch!' He spread his hands in an expansive gesture and considered her solemn face, then gave a resigned shrug. 'Not convinced by kismet, eh? Nellie, gents' outfitting is like a ghost town. Haven't had a customer — or even a time-wasting browser — since we opened. It was driving me up the wall. Standing there like one of the tailor's dummies, hoping and praying somebody would come up the stairs and buy a pair of socks.'

'You mean you just walked off the floor and came up here to read the paper and have a smoke?' she hissed incredulously, her eyes wide. 'What on earth did Mr Poppleton say?'

Brian gave a snort of laughter. 'Old

Popinjay's at a hospital appointment with his gimpy leg. Probably be gone the whole day.'

'That's no excuse for abandoning your station, Brian!' she persisted. 'You shouldn't have done it. It's not right!'

'You worry too much, Nellie,' he remarked easily. 'Anyhow, it isn't like I left the floor unmanned. The lad is up there, dusting shelves and polishing the mirrors. If a customer should happen to wander in, he's more than capable of selling them a box of hankies.'

'That's hardly the point.' She sat back in her chair, her forehead creasing. 'What do you imagine Mr Poppleton will say when he finds out?'

'Popinjay won't find out,' returned Brian confidently, gathering up his cup and plate. 'I slipped the lad a couple of bob to keep mum, so nobody'll ever be any the wiser. Now, are you eating today or what?'

Ellen shook her head, frustrated at not being able to get through to Brian. If any of the management — or, worse, one of the Hathersedges — spotted him away from his post without permission, he'd be sacked on the spot. 'I'm taking a sandwich upstairs. I need to type up the notes from this morning's meeting before Mr Mark gets back.'

'You've surely time for a cup of tea? Not even Mr Mark would begrudge you that!' chided Brian, starting from the table. 'Tell you what. We'll have a cuppa together, then I'll sneak back to gents' outfitting and not budge again until knocking-off time. Scout's honour!'

Ellen glanced over her shoulder, watching him sauntering between the tables down towards the counter. He was a tall man, powerfully-built and lithe of movement. Although the smart business suit and crisp white shirt had been bought second-hand, they fitted Brian's broad-shouldered frame as though tailor-made. The canteen was starting to fill up for the second sitting, and Ellen wasn't blind to the admiring glances Brian was attracting from the sales girls crowding into the lunch queue. She couldn't suppress a thrill of possessive pride that Brian never ever had eyes for any girl but her.

He returned a few minutes later and set the wooden tray down upon the table, sitting back and watching Ellen as she removed the cups and saucers.

'The derby scone is for you,' he said, his full lips parting in a wry grin. 'You need some nourishment in the middle of the working day. Besides, I happen to recall you're partial to a nice derby scone!'

Their eyes met, and despite her concerns over Brian's bunking off from his floor, Ellen relaxed and couldn't help smiling. They'd met when she'd wandered into a bakery on Dean Street in search of scones for tea, and wishing to order an iced cake to take home to Yorkshire for her mother's birthday. Brian had been behind the counter and she'd assumed he was the baker. He'd let her go on believing that, listening attentively to her detailed instructions for the birthday cake. It wasn't until he'd personally delivered a beautifully-iced and -decorated jam-and-cream sponge to her lodgings, and asked Ellen out, that Brian confessed he knew nothing about cakes and had only been helping out behind the counter of his friend's bakery while on leave from the Navy.

'Thanks for the scone,' she said, eyeing the vanilla slice on his plate. 'Can we eat up quickly and get back to work?'

'Can't wait!' he cried. 'All those shirts, ties and woolly pullovers . . . bliss!'

Reaching across the table, he touched her cheek with his fingertips. 'Me coming up here for a sly cuppa . . . I wouldn't have done it if there'd been any chance of getting found out, Nellie. I don't take daft risks. This certainly isn't the job of my dreams, but it's the best I've had since I come ashore, and I wouldn't have got it if you hadn't stuck your neck out and grovelled to old Popinjay. I am grateful, queen.'

'It's a decent job, Brian,' she responded sensibly. 'There are prospects. And security. Mr Poppleton started as a delivery boy in the Food Hall and has worked his way up to department manager. He'll have a jolly good pension when he retires, too. Hathersedge's treats its employees very fairly.'

Brian said nothing. Just sat, his chin cupped into his hand, gazing across at her.

'What?' she queried at last. 'Why are you looking at me like that?'

'Just thinking how lucky I am to have you,' he murmured simply, taking her hand into his. 'These past months have been rough, but finally I can see some light at the end of the tunnel.

'Everything's going to be alright from now on, Nellie — I know it!' he gave her a jaunty wink, gathering up his cup and plate before rising from the table and bestowing a chaste kiss upon her cheek. 'I'm off to work. Enjoy the rest of your scone!'

'I will — oh, Brian — ' She smiled up at him, asking as an afterthought: 'Where's your letter from? I saw a very fancy foreign stamp!'

'The Caribbean, no less!' he grinned.

'An old shipmate bringing me up to date with all his news. I wanted a bit of peace and quiet to read it, so I came up here. His ship's due back in Liverpool soon, so you'll meet him then. You'll like old Roger.' He started away, turning sharply on his heel to look back. 'How about I come over on Sunday for dinner? I'll tidy up Mrs Cummings' garden while I'm at it. What are you doing tonight?'

She gazed at him, crestfallen. 'Hilary and I are going to the pictures! But you're more than welcome to join us — Hilary won't mind.'

'What are you going to see?' he asked suspiciously.

'Betty Grable. It's — '

'Whoa — I can't stand all that singing and dancing!' he interrupted. 'Thanks all the same, but count me out. We'll go dancing tomorrow night instead.'

'That'd be grand!'

'It's a date.' He blew her a kiss. 'See you then, queen!'

# 2

A few Sundays later, Ellen and Hilary were strolling home from church; as soon as they turned into Laburnum Avenue, they spotted Brian clipping the privet in Mrs Cummings' garden.

'It's marvellous seeing Brian around the house again,' smiled Hilary. 'Mrs Cummings is delighted at having him back, too! Before we left for church, I couldn't help noticing she was making his favourite for afters!'

'Marmalade pud and evaporated milk! Yes, I noticed that too,' laughed Ellen, adding quietly: 'Everything's perfect between us. Just like it used to be.'

A little later, they were sitting in the back garden scraping carrots and peeling potatoes for the Sunday dinner. Ellen worked thoughtfully, watching Brian as he strode up and down mowing the grass.

'A penny for them!' remarked Hilary.

'I really want Ma and Jeanette to meet Brian. I want him to get to know my family and see my home,' replied Ellen. 'Whenever he was on leave, I'd suggest we take a trip up to Whinforth. Brian never actually *refused*, but somehow he always managed to put it off.'

'He wouldn't be the first young man who was nervous about meeting his sweetheart's family,' reflected Hilary. 'Bernard dilly-dallied for the longest while. It took him months to pluck up sufficient courage to have *that* conversation with my father!'

'Somehow, I can't imagine Brian being bashful about anything!' went on Ellen. 'I know Whinforth is miles away and it takes forever to get there, but Ma's birthday is coming up, and . . .'

'It was Dorothy's birthday that brought you and Brian together,' chipped in Hilary. 'How well I recall this incredibly handsome man with the winning smile turning up on Mrs Cummings' doorstep, carrying an enormous box containing the biggest, most spectacularly-decorated birthday cake I'd ever set eyes upon!'

Ellen was laughing now, recalling those first heady days when she'd met Brian and been unable to think about little else but when she'd see him again!

'Do you remember the performance we had trying to keep the box upright and not let it get squashed on the journey to Whinforth?' Hilary asked, shaking her head. 'That crowded train from Lime Street with only one empty seat, and we took turns sitting down with the box wedged on our lap!'

'Oh, the train was heaven compared to that bus full of schoolchildren! Standing room only, and jammed in like sardines the whole way. How Ma's cake didn't end up a boxful of crumbs, I'll never know!'

'It was worth every moment, though, wasn't it?' reflected Hilary affectionately. Apart from an elder brother in Derbyshire, her family were all gone, and in the years since she and Ellen had been friends, she'd become extremely fond of Ellen's mother and younger sister. 'It was a magnificent cake, and Dorothy's face was an absolute picture when she opened the box and saw it!'

'I want Brian to be part of those sort of memories,' Ellen said softly. 'Should I ask him to come with us to Whinforth for Ma's birthday?'

'Wouldn't Brian feel left out if you *didn't* invite him?'

'I hadn't thought of it like that,' admitted Ellen. 'It's only that everything's going along so well just now, I don't want to spoil it by rushing him.'

'It's only right and proper Brian meet your family, and there really isn't any excuse for him not to make the effort to do so,' commented Hilary firmly. 'You know, in all the time you and Brian have been courting, I can't recall him ever once mentioning his own family. How extraordinary!'

'He never speaks of them,' answered Ellen soberly. 'When we first starting going out, I asked him about his family, and all he'd say was they didn't get along. He left home at fifteen and hasn't seen them since.'

'How terribly sad!' exclaimed Hilary. 'You and I are very fortunate in coming from close and happy families, Nell.'

Ellen nodded, chewing her lip thoughtfully. 'I'll invite Brian this afternoon.'

'Good! You might well be surprised at his response!' replied Hilary. 'It's going to be a fine day. Are you going anywhere nice?'

'Christie Park. They've boats on the lake again for the first time since the war, so Brian's taking me rowing!' she laughed. 'Then we'll have a walk around the flower gardens and listen to the band at the pavilion.'

* ★ *

'..I've been thinking about Hilary,' remarked Ellen, when she and Brian were strolling through the park towards the lake. 'It's so unfair she's on her own! I mean, Ma lost Dad, and he was far too young to die, but at least they'd had nearly thirty years of happiness. Hilary and her husband spent only a few weeks of their marriage together!'

'I know it sounds heartless, Nellie, but it's a fact of war,' commented Brian, flagging down the ice-cream man's bicycle and buying two cornets. 'Nothing's ever the same as it was before.'

Ellen sighed, then turned to him curiously. 'What did you do before the war, Brian? You never speak of those times.'

'Not much to tell, queen. A painter and decorator give me a job when I was fourteen.' He slipped an arm about her shoulders. 'Later he took me on as an apprentice, and I served my time. But for old Adolf, I'd probably still be there!'

Their eyes met and they stole a kiss, moving closer. After a moment, Ellen opened her eyes and gazed up at him.

'Brian, it's Ma's birthday soon,' she began quietly. 'Hilary and I always try to take a few days' holiday from work so we can go up to Whinforth for a few days.'

'Sounds nice.'

'You've only just started at Hathersedge's, so you can't take any time off, but perhaps you could come just for the day? Catch the train after work on Saturday, spend Sunday with us and then travel back overnight? I realise it's a horrendously long journey, and you'd have work first thing Monday morning, but — '

'Hey, don't fuss! It's a great idea!' he responded. 'I'll ask Popinjay if I can have some time off. When I explain I want to visit your mam on her birthday, he's bound to bend the rules and let me go!'

'Don't get into any trouble!' she warned in dismay.

'You worry too much, Nellie!' He dropped a kiss onto the top of her head. 'You'll have to tell me what prezzie to get your mam. And what about the cake? Have you and Hilary got it sorted out?'

'Not yet. You were at sea last year, but we went back to your friend's bakery.'

'Nick does knock up a good cake, doesn't he?' grinned Brian, surprising Ellen with his enthusiasm. 'Why don't I sort the cake out? My contribution to the celebrations. It'll be great seeing Nick again, too. I haven't bumped into to him since I did that stint helping out.'

'It was purest chance I went into his bakery that day,' mused Ellen, her head against Brian's shoulder. 'Hilary recommended it. It's just across the road from the insurance company, so she goes there for the office elevenses.'

'Good location for a bakery, that,' considered Brian. 'With all them offices round about. Nick had the right idea, you know. He'd been a chef at a big hotel in Southport. He always said, once the war was over, he'd be out of the Navy like a shot and start up his own business.'

'He seems to be doing very well,' commented Ellen. 'The bakery's always busy.'

'That's the thing, you know,' went on

Brian, as the lake came into view. 'Start your own business. Be your own boss. None of this yes sir, no sir, three bags full sir!'

Several people were already out on the water, and in the shallows close to the bank, small boys and their fathers were racing wooden boats with hand-kerchief sails.

Brian helped Ellen aboard a brightly painted rowboat and took the oars, cutting into the clear water with smooth strokes so the little craft glided away from the jetty. 'Thank you for bringing me here,' murmured Ellen contentedly, trailing her fingertips in the cool water. 'This is a real treat.'

'Glad you're enjoying it.' He raised the oars, allowing the boat to drift. 'It's nice feeling the swell of water again — even if it is only a boating lake!'

'Do you miss the sea very much?' she asked, narrowing her eyes to make out his face through the sunshine.

'Yeah, I suppose I do. In a way. I knew my job, and I was good at it, and

I got respect for doing it. That's important to a man, Nellie. I didn't understand it then, but I do now.'

She drew a slow breath, hesitating before asking, 'Do you regret coming ashore?'

'No! No, 'course I don't, queen!' He reached forward and clasped her hand. 'It was time for me to leave the Navy and start a new life with you. Where I went wrong was rushing into it. Not making any proper plans for when I got off that ship for the last time.'

'As Nick did with his bakery, you mean?'

'Exactly. Or like Roger — you remember me mentioning Rodge? He got out right after the war. Did a couple of commercial runs back and forth to New York, then landed a plum job on a cruiser! One of them luxury liners full of nobs with money to burn. He's never looked back. Even does a bit of freelance work on the side now. Skippering ritzy little parties on fishing trips and holidays and such. Money for old rope, he reckons. Makes a lot of useful contacts that way, too.

'Had another letter from him, you know,' Brian reflected, gazing beyond Ellen into the distance. 'He's got big plans for the future. Said he's looking forward to us getting together next time he's in town. Suggested we go out for a slap-up dinner somewhere fancy — that's Rodge all over! Everything in style!'

'I'll look forward to meeting him,' remarked Ellen quietly. With his old shipmates doing so spectacularly well, small wonder Brian was restless and dissatisfied with his job in gents' outfitting!

'Perhaps we could make up a foursome, invite Hilary to come with us,' went on Brian, the distant look still in his eyes. 'But don't go getting any ideas about matchmaking — Rodge is the footloose and fancy-free type!'

Their conversation fell silent, the creak of the oars and plash of water keeping them company as they returned to the jetty. Wandering hand in hand through the flower gardens, they bought a pot of tea from the kiosk and took it to the seats set out around the bandstand.

'I wish we could be married right now,' Brian said unexpectedly. 'But I've nothing to offer you.'

'That's nonsense!' she cried, adding with a shy smile: 'Two can live as cheaply as one, you know!'

'That's rubbish, queen,' he retorted abruptly. 'I've seen what scratching for every penny does to people. It tears them apart until nothing's left.'

'Brian — ' she protested, her eyes filled with dismay.

'No, I want the best for you,' he interrupted fiercely as the musicians took their places on the bandstand. 'I'm going to make something of myself, Nellie — I promise you that!'

# 3

'In a way, it's a shame we're off to Yorkshire just now,' began Ellen guilelessly, glancing sidelong at Hilary when they were packing for their trip. 'While Roger is still in Liverpool. If we weren't going away for the week, I daresay we would've all had another night out together, wouldn't we?'

'Mmm,' replied Hilary, checking the contents of her small suitcase against a neatly written list. 'I daresay.'

'We *did* have a very pleasant evening, didn't we?' persisted Ellen in exasperation. 'A scrumptious dinner and then dancing at that gorgeous hotel.'

'Yes.' Hilary frowned, glancing around the room. 'I'm sure I've forgotten something important!'

'Are you going to see him again or not?' asked Ellen bluntly.

'Roger?' she remarked vaguely, still

frowning over the list. 'Don't expect so. Why would I?'

'You seemed to get along very well,' prompted Ellen impatiently.

'I suppose we did rather,' considered Hilary, pausing in her packing. 'Yes, I enjoyed our conversation very much. Roger's a nice man.'

'Handsome, too,' pressed Ellen. 'Perhaps he'll still be here when we get back!'

'Nell! Stop trying to fix me up,' admonished Hilary. 'Besides, I happen to know Roger's leaving tomorrow. He's skippering for a party of American tourists, I believe.'

'Ah ha! So you *are* interested in his comings and goings!'

Hilary aimed a cushion at her friend. 'Do something useful and sit on my case while I fasten it — although I'm certain I've left something out!'

★　★　★

That evening, Ellen had no sooner arrived home then she heard Hilary's key in the front door.

'Hi! We're in the kitchen!' she called excitedly. 'Brian's left the cake!'

'He brought it over at dinnertime. Couldn't stay for a cuppa, though,' explained Mrs Cummings, when the three were gathered around the kitchen table. Ellen was carefully snipping the string and opening the large cardboard box.

'Said he'd picked the cake up during his lunch hour and was in a hurry to get back to work,' went on their landlady. 'Said to tell you he'd meet you both at the station. Under the big clock at seven sharp. What time's your train?'

'Not 'til five to eight,' answered Ellen, easing off the box's lid. 'But that train's always packed, so we need to be really early to be sure of getting seats.'

'Especially with a fragile birthday cake to — ' chuckled Hilary, breaking off when the lid was finally removed and the cake revealed. 'Oh, Nell! It's glorious! Brian's baker pal has excelled himself.'

'Prettiest cake I've ever seen, and no mistake!' declared Mrs Cummings. 'Your mam'll be thrilled to bits, Nellie. My, just look at the work that's gone into making all those delicate little sugar flowers and leaves — it'll be a shame to cut into it!'

'It is magnificent, isn't it? Brian said he'd ask Nick to make something extra-special,' beamed Ellen, her cheeks pink. 'Now all we have to do is get it to Whinforth in one piece — at least this year we'll have Brian to help us!'

'Isn't it lucky Brian's able to take tomorrow off?' Hilary said when they were approaching Lime Street train station, their pace slowing on the steeply-sloping cobbles. 'Now he'll be able to spend the whole weekend in Whinforth.'

'He wasn't entitled to a day off, but I'm afraid he prevailed upon Mr Poppleton's good nature,' admitted Ellen ruefully. 'It's almost seven,' she went on, glancing up to the huge clock face the instant they turned into the

33

station. 'I can't see him anywhere, can you?'

Hilary searched the mass of people milling around the smoky, dimly-lit station and shook her head. 'Let's put the bags down over in that corner and wait there. We'll have a clear view of the entrance and spot Brian as soon as he comes in. There's still heaps of time.'

However, when another ten minutes had ticked away and there was still no sign of him, Ellen began to get fidgety. 'He should be here by now. Look at the length of the queue building up at the ticket office. It'll take ages just to get our tickets! Where on earth can he be? He told Mrs Cummings he'd be here at seven sharp.'

'He's probably been delayed,' reassured Hilary. 'Perhaps he's had to stay a little late at Hathersedge's.'

'Maybe.' Ellen chewed her lip, unconvinced.

'Why don't you stay here with the bags and keep watch for him, while I get into the queue for our tickets?'

However even by the time Hilary returned from the ticket office, Brian still had not arrived. 'I can't just stand around waiting! Something's wrong, I can feel it,' fretted Ellen. 'The train's already filling up, let's bag seats and get our luggage aboard. Then you sit tight, while I go to Brian's digs and find out what's happened. He was going back there after work to collect his things.'

Seated in the carriage, the cake box on her lap, Hilary glanced uneasily at the younger woman as she stowed their cases up onto the luggage rack. 'You've never been to Brian's lodgings before. It's a rough quarter down there by the docks, and it's getting dark. You shouldn't go alone.'

'Don't worry, Hilary, I'm taking a taxi. I'll have to: there isn't time to do otherwise.' She pushed open the compartment door. 'At least I'll find out what's going on. Wish me luck!'

The hackney cab wound away from the station and across the heart of the city, cutting down into the docklands where towering courts and ranks of two-up-two-down dwellings were crammed into rows and rows of long, narrow streets. There were few streetlamps. Alleys and corners were thick with shadow and Ellen was mightily relieved she wasn't on foot and alone.

'I think this must be it, just ahead to the left,' she said at last, leaning from the cab's window. 'I can't see the numbers on the doors, but I recall mention of the house being near the tanners' yard.'

'Are you sure you want to get out here, miss?' sniffed the driver morosely.

'I'm collecting my fiancé and going back to the station. We're catching the train at five to eight.'

'Have to get a move on, then.'

'Will you wait here for me, please?' she asked, alighting and hurrying to a battered door. Knocking urgently, she stood back, looking up at the house and wondering which room was Brian's. In the upper window, a dingy light burned behind torn curtains that didn't quite meet in the centre. Agitated and anxious, Ellen peered in at the downstairs window. Light was showing from a back room, but there was no sign of anybody coming to answer the door. She knocked again, harder and longer, bruising her knuckles on the scarred paint. Impatience and desperation were biting deep, and Ellen raised her fist to thump on the door when it was wrenched open.

'What d'yer think yer doin'?' demanded a fat man, shoving his flabby face close to hers as he lunged out, but stopping dead when he saw the waiting taxi driver. 'What d'yer want?'

Ellen involuntarily took a step backwards, but raised her chin and stared up at him. 'I'm here to see Brian Kennedy, if you'll kindly show me to his room.'

'Yer out o' luck.' The man wiped the back of his hand across his mouth. 'He's not 'ere.'

A frisson of alarm shot up Ellen's spine. 'Has he been in from work?' she demanded.

The fat man shrugged, eyeing her craftily.

'You must know if he came into the house this evening!' she blurted in exasperation, then suddenly realised what he was about and, reaching into her handbag, cautiously withdrew her purse. 'I'd be obliged if you could help me.'

'Yer shoulda said.' He ran the tip of his tongue over flaccid lips. 'He come in from work like usual.'

'But he went out again,' she murmured, her heart pounding. 'Was he going to the train station?'

He shrugged again, and Ellen made another offering while the taxi driver honked his horn impatiently.

'Some bloke come to see him and they went out together.'

'Do you know where they were going? What did this man look like?'

The fat man shrugged again, but this time Ellen held the silver coins out of reach. 'Tell me what the man was like, and then I want to see Brian's room.'

'Tall. Flash. Fancied 'imself a right Lord Muck.' The landlord snatched at the money and stood aside for Ellen to enter the squalid dwelling. 'Room's up at the back.'

The steep, narrow stairs were unlit and Ellen groped at the rail to guide her way. The smoky gas lamp burning in the front room cast murky light through the open doorway and onto the landing, so she found Brian's door easily enough. There was no lock or key, and she turned the knob and pushed it wide open, stepping into a narrow shoebox of a room with one small, curtainless window and a low, sagging bed.

Shock and confusion blurred her senses. How could Brian live in an awful place like this? Why did he, when he was able to afford somewhere clean and decent? Ellen's mind was reeling, then in the dingy light she spotted Brian's kitbag, packed and tied and ready to go. He'd left it behind.

Running down the stairs, there was

no sign of the fat man, so she turned toward the rear of the house and looked in at the back room. He was there. Seated at a dirty table eating from a newspaper.

'Did they go to the Seamen's Mission?'

He shrugged again, but this time Ellen merely turned on her heel and sped from the fetid house, slamming the door shut behind her.

Clambering into the taxi, she leaned forward. 'The Seamen's Mission, please. The one in the bombed-out church.'

'I know where it is, miss,' replied the driver, glancing over his shoulder. 'But you'll never make it, if you're still set on catching that train! We'll only just get there if we head back to Lime Street right now.'

'The station then, thank you,' Ellen replied at once, falling back into the leather seat, her mind a turmoil of confusion and disbelief. Whyever had Brian gone out with Roger, when he should have been on his way to catch the Yorkshire train?

Ellen reached Lime Street with only six minutes to spare, racing along the platform towards the carriage. Hilary met her at the compartment door, alarmed at her friend's troubled face.

'Brian was packed and ready,' Ellen got out breathlessly, 'but he went off with Roger! If he doesn't go back for his kitbag, he might still get here in time. I'm going to wait by the barrier. If I see Brian coming, I'll ask the guard to hold the train!'

'Be careful you don't — ' Hilary began, but Ellen was already sprinting away along the platform towards the ticket barriers. ' — miss it yourself . . . '

Returning to her seat, she peered from the compartment window, but Ellen's figure was obscured by the smoke and steam and fiery smuts and sparks belching forth from the train as the fireman stoked its engine.

Porters were running back and forth hauling laden trolleys; last-minute passengers were dashing through the

41

barriers and hurling themselves into the nearest carriage; the guard was pacing up and down the platform, consulting his pocket-watch and making last-minute checks before blowing the whistle that would signal the train on its long journey.

Ellen kept one eye upon him, but her attention never strayed from the station entrance, willing Brian to somehow emerge from the surging throng of travellers and run towards her. That familiar, lazy grin spreading across his face as he caught her up into his arms and launched into apologetic explanations.

Carriage doors were slamming. Ellen saw Hilary waving frantically. The final whistle blew.

'All aboard who's going aboard!'

Glancing over her shoulder at the station clock, Ellen turned and sped through the thick clouds of steam and smoke billowing along the platform as the train rumbled into life. The noise was deafening. Ellen couldn't even hear the sound of her footsteps. Only the aching thump of her heart inside her chest as she ran for all she was worth, tears blinding her eyes as she finally grasped the handle and hauled herself up into the carriage.

# 4

The journey from Liverpool to Whinforth — clear across Lancashire, over
the Pennines and north-easterly up
through Yorkshire — was long and
convoluted, complicated by several
changes between trains, trams and
buses. It was almost daylight when the
battered boneshaker trundled over
the Dow Hills and down around steep,
twisting roads into the medieval wool
town. Veering around a sharp corner,
the bus finally shuddered to a halt on
the worn cobbles surrounding the
Great War memorial.

'Home at last!' sighed Ellen, as they
walked through deserted, gas-lit streets
towards the Butterworths' corner shop
and the tall house behind it where the
family lived. 'Look at the sky — it's
going to be fine weather for Ma's
birthday!'

At long last, they turned onto Market Street and the corner shop came into their sights. There was a soft light glowing behind the curtains at the window of Ellen's room, directly above the shop. Going around the side and through the arched ginnel, they'd no sooner let themselves into the back yard than the kitchen door opened and Dorothy Butterworth hurried out to welcome them, drying her hands on her apron and bustling the two women indoors.

'Happy birthday, Ma!' beamed Ellen, setting the cake box down onto the dresser so she might wrap her arms about her mother's thin shoulders. 'You haven't seen this box and you've no idea what might be inside it!'

'And which box might that be?' chuckled Dorothy, turning to hug Hilary. 'Hello, pet! My, but it's grand to see you again!'

She glanced questioningly at Ellen. 'Is Brian not with you?'

Ellen turned away, taking off her

coat. 'He was keen to come, but at the last minute couldn't make the train.'

'Oh, what a pity! We were so looking forward to meeting him,' Dorothy responded sympathetically. 'Still, never mind, there'll be lots of other times, I'm sure.

'You'll be cold, hungry and tired after that awful journey. I've some breakfast keeping hot on the stove, and Jeanette baked yesterday so the bread's nice and crusty,' she went on, disappearing into the hallway with their coats. 'Then you can get straight to your beds — there'll be time enough for catching up later!'

Ellen's old room was ready and waiting for them. Jeanette had lit the fire and it was burning brightly in the small grate, casting warm shadows across the floral-papered walls. Hilary was sitting up in bed, tying back her hair ready to cream her face; however, Ellen was in the window seat, her legs tucked beneath her, staring out across the empty street.

'What do you think Ma made of

Brian's not being with us?' she murmured at last. 'She asked about him as soon as we got here. Do you think she thinks it's queer he hasn't come?'

'Why would she?' replied Hilary gently. During their journey north, Ellen hadn't spoken of whatever had occurred at Brian's lodgings. Hilary hadn't questioned her, certain the younger woman would confide when she wished to do so. 'Naturally, Dorothy was disappointed not to meet Brian — he's to be her son-in-law, after all — but there's nothing queer about something unforeseen cropping up, is there?'

'He's let me down for no good reason!' cried Ellen suddenly, spinning around with unshed tears glittering in her hazel eyes. 'Brian *knew* how much this visit means to me! He was packed and ready, but when Roger turned up he just swanned off goodness knows where! Going for a night out with his old shipmate was obviously more important than coming home with me to meet my family and celebrate Ma's birthday with us!'

'You can't possibly be certain of that, Nell!' exclaimed Hilary, pausing with the open pot of vanishing cream in her hands. 'You won't know what's happened until you've spoken to Brian. One thing is certain, he would never deliberately let you down.'

'But that's exactly what he *has* done!' argued Ellen, getting up from the window seat and tossing her hair brush onto the chest of drawers before punching her pillows into a hollow and flopping onto the bed. 'I was upset and disappointed at first, but now I feel so — so *angry*! I only come home to Whinforth at Christmas and for birthdays, yet Brian couldn't be bothered making an effort and keeping his promise!'

Hilary smoothed the vanishing cream into her skin. 'Don't be too hasty making judgement until you've actually heard Brian's side of it,' she advised. 'If he could've let you know not to wait at the station, I'm sure he would have done so. And if the shop had a telephone, I've no doubt Brian would've already called to explain everything. And apologise profusely.'

'You really think so?' ventured Ellen doubtfully.

'Yes, I do. He may even catch this morning's early mail train from Lime Street. Just because Brian missed one train doesn't mean he can't catch another.'

A less troubled expression settled upon Ellen's face and she snuggled further into her bed, warming her cold toes on the stone hot water bottle. 'I hadn't thought about that. The first train will be leaving in a couple of hours.'

'That reminds me,' yawned Hilary, also settling down. 'I told your mum we'd see to the papers so she and Jeanette can sleep late.'

'Call yourself a friend!' groaned Ellen, reaching for the heavy brass alarm clock. 'That was a thoughtful gesture, Hilary. Wish I'd thought of it. Poor Ma did look worn out, didn't she?'

'Hardly surprising.' Hilary burrowed deeper into the cosy flannelette sheets. 'I daresay she was up at the crack of dawn yesterday and has been on her feet ever since.'

'After Ma's had a nice lie-in this morning, I'll take her breakfast in bed and she's not to set foot in the shop all day long!' decided Ellen, switching off the bedside lamp and stretching languorously beneath the covers. 'Ooh, it's nice to be home! I wonder if Brian will turn up on the early train — it'll be wonderful if he does!'

'The icing on the cake, you mean?'

Ellen groaned, and with a smile closed her eyes.

★ ★ ★

Surprisingly, she slept like a top and was awake and out of bed with the alarm clock's first ring.

Ellen was opening the shop's doors as the paper van trundled around the corner onto Market Street, and she and Hilary were already making good progress marking up the newspapers, magazines and comics ready for the paperboys before the kettle finished boiling for the first cuppa of the day.

No sooner was the shop open than regular customers started coming in for their papers and smokes or sweets, and the tea was growing cold before the pair had time to drink it.

'Did you think Ma looked alright last night?' queried Ellen, hurriedly sorting the home deliveries into bundles ready for the paperboys. 'I don't just mean tired, but paler. Thinner, too.'

'Perhaps a little. It was the early hours of the morning, though. She must've been exhausted.'

'Ma's not getting any younger, Hilary. What if the shop's getting too much for her?' Ellen frowned. 'The drawback of a shop like this is that it's open all hours and every day of the week. Every day of the year, practically!'

'It's certainly a great deal of hard

work, even for two people working together — ' Hilary broke off as the first of the paperboys shambled in and collected his heavy delivery sack.

'Jeanette more than pulls her weight,' continued Ellen when they were alone once more. 'Not just for Ma's sake, but because she really loves this old shop. Always has. I remember asking her what she wanted to do when she grew — '

'Morning, all!' A little woman, round as a tub, with dark eyes bright as new buttons bustled into the shop, stopping in mid-step and exclaiming, 'Nellie! I should've guessed you'd be back for your ma's birthday! You're looking right bonny! At least they're feeding you proper down there in Liverpool!'

'Thanks, Mrs Heggie,' responded Ellen, suddenly feeling the size of a house next to Hilary's slender figure. 'Mr Munro's newspaper has already gone with the paperboy.'

'Nay, nay. It's my own stuff I'm after. I'll have my *Family Star*, the *Radio*

*Fun, Comic Cuts* and two ounces each of mint imperials, rosebuds and wine gums.'

'Shall I put the children's comics on Mr Munro's account, Mrs Heggie?' enquired Ellen, selecting the jars of sweets from the rows of shelves lining the walls of the well-stocked corner shop.

Ada shook her head vigorously. 'I get these for the bairns — my little treat! Nay, Mr Munro's not fussy on Peggy and Robbie having comics. I daresay I shouldn't get them, knowing their dad doesn't approve. Still, what he doesn't know won't harm him, and it seems to me a right shame the kiddies can't have a bit o' fun like their little friends do.'

'Why ever doesn't this man allow his children comics?' Hilary asked, looking up from tidying a display of stationery. 'I've heard comics can be a useful aid to children's reading.'

'Mr Munro is a serious sort,' explained Ada with a shake of her head. 'Don't get me wrong, he may be a mite old-fashioned and strict, but he means well. He lets them read story papers — little Robbie gets *The Rainbow* and Peggy has *Girls' Crystal* every week — and of course he gives them plenty of proper books, but he reckons the antics in comics set a bad example.'

'What does the children's mother think?' persisted Hilary.

'Mr Munro's a widower,' sighed the elderly woman. 'Sheelagh passed away after Robbie was born.'

'How very sad!' exclaimed Hilary, immediately sympathetic. 'Is he bringing up the children alone?'

'Oh, aye. He's no family round about. Him and the missus moved down here from the Borders,' she explained, digging deep into her worn purse. 'Oh, while you're there, Nellie, I'll take a packet of pipe-cleaners as well!'

'Taken up smoking a pipe, have you?' grinned Ellen, weighing up the sweeties and emptying them from the shining brass scoop into triangular little paper bags, twisting the tops tightly to keep the contents secure.

'Away with your daftness, Nellie!' Arranging the purchases in her basket, Ada turned away from the counter. 'Nice to see you both again. Give my best to your ma for her birthday, won't you?'

Hilary watched the little woman hurrying away towards the river. Market Street was filling up with people, bicycles, horse-drawn drays and carts. There still weren't very many motor cars to be seen on the steep, cobbled streets of the old town. 'I can't place this Mr Munro. Have I ever met him?'

'Hmm?' queried Ellen. She'd been thinking about Brian. Wondering if even now he was aboard the train from Lime Street and on his way to join her. 'Oh. Doubt it. I gather he keeps himself to himself. I don't know him either, except to say good-morning. The family moved to Whinforth long after I'd left, so I never even saw his wife.

'We should be fairly quiet for a while now until the kiddies start pouring in to get sweets for their Saturday morning pictures,' she went on, glancing at the clock. 'Will you hold the fort while I get Ma's breakfast on the go? If by chance there's a stampede, give me a shout and I'll come to the rescue!'

Climbing the flights of stairs with the breakfast tray carefully balanced in her arms, Ellen passed her young sister hurrying down.

'Welcome home, Nellie!' she cried, honey-blonde curls bobbing like a golden halo about her pretty, heart-shaped face. 'Thanks so much for taking over the papers so I could get some extra beauty sleep!'

'As if you need it!' laughed Ellen. 'I'm taking this in to Ma; your share is keeping hot downstairs.'

'Good-o!' she whooped, clattering down the rest of the stairs. 'I'm famished!'

When Ellen knocked and went into her mother's room at the top of the house, Dorothy was already awake.

'You're spoiling me, love!' she exclaimed, when Ellen settled the tray upon her lap. 'I could get used to sleeping late and having fancy breakfasts in bed!'

'It's about time you did!' returned Ellen, kissing her mother's cheek and perching on the edge of the bed. 'Happy birthday again! The yard'll be nice and sunny later. Why don't you take your new book and sit outside for a while? You could do with some roses in your cheeks!'

'I can't sit round all day doing nothing!'

'Course you can! Jeanette, Hilary and I will manage the shop,' replied Ellen, rising from the bed. 'We're making a special meal for this evening — so you're barred from the kitchen too!'

* * *

As midday passed and afternoon slipped away, Ellen tried to stop herself looking from the shop window at every opportunity in the hope she'd spot Brian striding along Market Street towards her.

57

He wasn't coming.

There was no point fooling herself any longer. He just wasn't going to come. Vainly trying to force thoughts of Brian from her mind, Ellen was pleased to see her mother reading a whodunit and enjoying the sunshine in the little whitewashed backyard.

As soon as the shop door closed for the night, Ellen, Jeanette and Hilary rolled up their sleeves and put on their aprons. Dorothy was banished to the comforts of the parlour with a pot of tea and the wireless until supper was ready.

For the next couple of hours, Ellen was far too preoccupied to dwell upon Brian's absence. The three women worked companionably and the delicious meal turned out well. They dressed the table with a fine linen cloth that was kept for special occasions and set out the family's best china. Hilary arranged posy bowls of yellow and violet flowers at each place, for the table's centrepiece would be the lavishly iced and decorated cake with its delicate candles in their rosebud cups.

Finally, all was ready. Dorothy was allowed out from the parlour, and while everyone gathered around the table, Ellen slipped into the pantry to fetch the cake and make a grand entrance. Standing there alone, poised to light the candles, a wave of uncertainty and melancholy suddenly washed over her. The cake had been Brian's contribution to the celebrations . . . Fiercely blinking back hot, foolish tears, Ellen struck a match, and with trembling hands set the little candles aflame.

Calling for Jeanette to turn out the light, Ellen pinned on a smile and sallied forth with the gorgeous cake.

'Happy Birthday, Ma!'

'And Many Happy Returns!'

Dorothy's pale face was glowing with happiness in the soft candlelight as she made her secret wish and took three attempts to blow out the tiny golden flames. Even as Ellen joined in the heartfelt good wishes and birthday song, she couldn't quite dispel the agitation gnawing deep within her. Why hadn't he come? Or at least written and got in touch?

Was this awful silence Brian's way of breaking up?

# 5

The days slid away, and all too quickly their holiday in Yorkshire was over. Ellen still hadn't heard from Brian, and somehow no longer expected to. Her heart was heavy with more than the usual sadness of saying goodbye to her mother and sister as she and Hilary trudged to the Great War memorial with their bags and boarded the ramshackle bus on the first leg of their journey back to Liverpool.

Although they had the train compartment to themselves for much of the time, Ellen wasn't inclined to discuss whatever news might be awaiting her when they reached Lime Street. She was sitting in a corner seat, elbow propped against the window ledge, hand cupping her chin, staring bleakly at the passing landscape as the miles chugged and rattled away.

Tactfully, Hilary hadn't disturbed her friend's troubled thoughts, and had settled to reading the Lord Peter Wimsey murder mystery Dorothy had lent her.

'It's not my place to go chasing after him, is it?' demanded Ellen, finally turning from the window as the train approached Lime Street. 'I should wait for Brian to explain himself, shouldn't I?'

Hilary glanced over the rims of her spectacles. 'Do I sense a 'but' coming?'

Ellen expelled a heavy sigh. 'I'm just so . . . weary . . . of thinking! About Brian. About his going off with Roger and leaving me in the lurch. About whether he's gone for good.'

'You're surely not thinking — oh no, Nell! You're *wrong!*' exclaimed Hilary in alarm. 'Brian loves you and wants to marry you. There's no doubt of that!'

'Isn't there?' she retorted softly.

'Nell, listen to me. This past week has been a tremendous strain for you. You've kept your concerns bottled up because you didn't want to spoil the celebrations and now you're thinking the very worst.'

Ellen shook her head miserably. 'I could've understood his missing the train, Hilary. But he's had nearly a whole week to scribble a note and put it in the post. If everything is still alright between us, why hasn't he been in touch?

'I'm just sick and tired of wondering and worrying,' she finished bleakly. 'I'm going to confront Brian and ask him straight out.'

Concern creased Hilary's forehead. 'Will you go to Brian's lodgings?'

'No fear! I never want to set foot in that awful place again, nor set eyes on that dreadful man,' she returned decisively. 'By the time we get into Liverpool, it'll be almost time for Brian to finish work. I'll go to Hathersedge's and wait for him.'

'Do you really think that's wise? Going to the store, I mean? Mightn't it be better to meet somewhere quiet, where you can talk in peace?'

Ellen shrugged. 'I'm certain of seeing him at Hathersedge's. I want this over and done — for better or worse!'

★ ★ ★

The train duly chugged to a shuddering halt alongside the platform at Lime Street, and the two friends climbed stiffly down from the carriage and started towards the ticket barrier. They'd been travelling since early morning and were exhausted, their bulging bags weighing them down.

'Hathersedge's won't be closing for almost an hour. Shall I wait with you, Nell?' enquired Hilary quietly. 'We could get a cup of tea.'

'No, thanks. I'd rather be by myself for a while,' replied Ellen with a resigned smile. 'I'll see you at home later.'

She decided against catching the bus across town to Hathersedge's. She couldn't face hauling her luggage onto a crowded bus. Besides, after so many hours travelling, she needed to stretch her legs. Balancing the bags evenly, Ellen started walking. Not briskly, for there was no point. There was plenty of time before Brian finished work.

Once at the store, Ellen went up to the staff canteen. It was empty, being so near closing time, and Beryl was alone wiping down the counter.

'I'm a little early meeting Brian.' Ellen smiled across at the canteen manager. 'Do you mind if I park myself and my bags here for a few minutes?'

'Course not!' Beryl gave her a long, curious look. 'I'll pour you a cuppa. Always have a brew myself last thing before heading home. There you go!'

'Thank you.' Ellen gratefully accepted the hot drink. 'I'm ready for this! It's been a long day. I've just got back from Yorkshire, visiting home.'

'Thought I hadn't seen you for a bit,' commented Beryl, studying the soggy dish cloth in her hands. 'I — er — I take it you haven't heard, then?'

Ellen's heart froze. 'Heard what?'

'It's not really for me to say,'

answered Beryl hastily, taken aback by Ellen's shocked expression. 'I only got it second-hand, anyhow.'

'What is it, Beryl? Tell me. Please!'

The other woman shrugged. 'There's been ructions. So I heard. There was talk over your feller getting given a day off, even though he hasn't been here five minutes, and how it wasn't fair and he shouldn't have got it. Anyhow, he should've come back to work on the Monday, but — '

Beryl broke off, falling silent as the canteen doors swung open and Mark Hathersedge stood on the threshold.

'Ah, Miss Butterworth! I was informed you were on the premises.' His greeting was cold. 'I trust you enjoyed your holiday?'

'Very much, thank you,' she answered, noticing Beryl turning her back to vigorously scrub at the sink. 'I — er — I'm waiting for Brian to finish work.'

'Your fiancé is no longer at Hathersedge's, Miss Butterworth.'

'What? I don't — '

'A word in my office, if you please.'

Turning on his heel, Mark Hathersedge strode smartly along the corridor, leaving Ellen to scramble to her feet, gather up her luggage and, with a bewildered glance at Beryl, hurry after her employer.

Dropping her bags beside her own desk, she followed Mark Hathersedge into his office.

'Miss Butterworth, your fiancé was given permission to take one day's leave so he might join you at a family celebration in Yorkshire. Am I correct in assuming that to be so?'

'Yes. Yes, of course,' she answered, mystified. 'It was my mother's birthday.'

'I'm sure you realise it was only out of respect for you that Mr Poppleton agreed to your fiancé's request?'

'Of course, and I was very grateful,' she replied in confusion. 'I'm sorry, but I don't understand any of this. Downstairs, you said Brian doesn't work here anymore . . .'

'Mr Kennedy has been dismissed. He failed to appear for work last Monday morning and has not had the courtesy to contact us concerning his absence,' answered Mark Hathersedge crisply, his narrowed eyes boring into her. 'Hathersedge's employed this man at your recommendation, Miss Butterworth. We would therefore be obliged for an explanation.'

Ellen stared at him, her thoughts racing. Something must be badly wrong. Brian wouldn't just disappear without a word. Suppose, after he'd left his digs with Roger, there'd been an accident? Or he'd been taken ill —

'Miss Butterworth?' Mark Hathersedge's clear voice cut through her panic. 'Are you quite well?'

'I'm sorry, sir. I knew nothing of this. Brian didn't come to Yorkshire. I thought he'd gone off for a night out with Roger and missed the train, but if he hasn't been into work . . . ' she babbled agitatedly, scrambling to her feet and grabbing up her bags.

'Miss Butterworth — '

Ellen was already gone.

Her head was spinning, and the fear that Brian might have come to harm gripped so tightly she could scarcely breathe. What to do! *What to do?* She clattered down the staircase, through the store and out onto the street. Brian's digs? No. No, she'd go home first. Talk to Hilary and Mrs Cummings. The landlady might even have seen Brian and know if he was safe and well . . .

Letting herself in at Laburnum Avenue, Ellen was dumping her bags at the foot of the stairs when she caught sight of Hilary bringing washing in from the back garden.

'Good heavens, Nell!' she cried, dropping the wash-basket as Ellen cannoned into the kitchen, her face ashen. 'Whatever's wrong?'

'It's Brian!' she blurted, her eyes huge and scared.

Neither of them heard the front door bell, nor Mrs Cummings emerge from the sitting-room and call down the hall:

'I'll get it!'

Before Ellen could begin explaining,

the landlady hurried into the kitchen, her face creased in smiles and her arms laden with a gigantic bouquet and an enormous box of chocolates.

'For you, Nellie!' exclaimed Mrs Cummings. 'My word, that lad thinks the world of you — I've not seen chocs like these since before the war, and not often even then!'

'For me?' echoed Ellen blankly.

'That's what the delivery boy said!' chuckled Mrs Cummings, pressing the gifts into Ellen's arms. 'There's a card, too. Open it up and see what he says. Eee, I love a bit of old-fashioned romance! You're a lucky lass, Nellie!'

Mechanically, Ellen withdrew a small envelope from the bouquet and glanced at the card. The instinctive surge of relief and joy was abruptly quashed when she read over the lines again, the words gradually coming into stark focus.

*Really, really sorry, Nellie. Couldn't be helped. Explain when I see you. Brian.*

'Short and sweet!' She passed the

card to Hilary, her voice barely audible. 'He didn't even bother to write it himself!'

' — don't think we've any vases big enough!' Mrs Cummings was saying, her remark muffled as she bent to rummage through the cupboard under the sink. 'You've a lot of flowers in that bouquet!'

'Why don't we divide them?' suggested Ellen, suddenly utterly composed. 'Hilary and I will take some upstairs, and you have the others down here for the sitting-room?'

'Are you sure? That's kind of you!' said Mrs Cummings, pleased. 'I'll fetch those big water jugs from the sideboard — they should be tall enough for the long stems.'

When she'd disappeared along the hall, Ellen rounded on Hilary, her face flushed and her eyes blazing. 'Can you believe that card? I've been worried sick, imagining all sorts of horrible things and thinking Brian might be ill or hurt, and he sends *that!*'

'Whatever's going on?' queried Hilary. 'You were frantic when you came in. Did you see Brian at Hathersedge's?'

'You don't know the half of it!' returned Ellen bitterly, launching into a rapid explanation.

'I can hardly believe it!' commented Hilary, when she'd heard what had occurred at the department store. 'I'd never have thought Brian to be so selfish.'

'Nor I!' concurred Ellen grimly. 'Hathersedge's may well be a stuffy old-fashioned firm like Brian says, but they're fair and decent employers and I've worked hard and done well there.'

'None of this is your fault,' began Hilary soberly. 'But unfortunately, Brian's behaviour does reflect badly upon you in the firm's eyes.'

'They hold me responsible. I was his referee. I gave Hathersedge's my word Brian was trustworthy and reliable!' she fumed, flicking the card into the pedal bin. 'I'm lucky to still have my own job, and Brian thinks a bunch of flowers and a box of chocolates makes what he's done alright!'

'At least he has apologised and promised you a proper explanation,' reasoned Hilary. 'He's obviously trying to make amends.'

Ellen was scarcely listening, her thoughts ticking over nineteen-to-the-dozen. 'You know, there's something very queer about all this! Brian hasn't had a penny in wages since the week before we went to Whinforth. And by leaving Hathersedge's without a word, he's forfeited anything owed to him in lieu of proper notice.

'Yet these flowers and chocolates must've cost a fortune, so how has he afforded them?' she brooded suspiciously, meeting her friend's gaze. 'What on earth is he up to, Hilary?'

# 6

It was another four evenings before Brian Kennedy rang the doorbell of Laburnum Avenue and was welcomed indoors by Mrs Cummings, who knew only of the flowers and chocolates but nothing of the discord that lay behind them.

'Come in, love!' she exclaimed, shepherding him into the sitting-room. 'Nellie should be back from work soon. Make yourself at home. Turn on the wireless, if you like. I've just taken a batch of currant buns from the oven, so I'll fetch you a couple and some tea to wash them down — I daresay you're hungry!'

'Now you mention it, I am a bit peckish!' he grinned, taking the easy chair at the fireplace. 'Mind you, I can never say 'no' to your baking!'

Ellen was exhausted when she got

home. She wasn't sleeping well, and where once she'd enjoyed her work, now each day was an ordeal. She couldn't help but be aware of the sly looks and wagging tongues wherever she went in the store. Hathersedge's was quite a close-knit community and gossip spread like wildfire. It seemed everybody knew Brian had disappeared and left her standing at the train station. There were even whispers he'd jilted Ellen on the eve of a secret wedding. It was awful, and she'd rarely felt so miserable. She wasn't sure which was hardest to take, the outrageous rumours or the genuine sympathy from well-meaning friends.

'Guess who's here, love!' called Mrs Cummings cheerily, popping her head around from the kitchen when Ellen opened the front door. 'He's in the sitting-room listening to the wireless. I'll bring in a pot of fresh tea, shall I?'

'No, thank you, Mrs Cummings.' Ellen tried to smile but couldn't quite manage it. Her heart was suddenly hammering uncomfortably. 'He — he won't be staying long.'

Hanging up her coat, she stood alone in the hall. She'd wanted to face Brian with her questions; however, now the moment had come, Ellen was scared what the answers might be. Gulping in a deep breath, she slowly outstretched her hand towards the sitting-room door, but even as she hesitated, it was pulled open and Brian Kennedy confronted her; the lazy, familiar smile spreading across his tanned face as he came forward to take Ellen into his arms.

'Ah, Nellie! It's great to see you — '

Stiff-backed, she sidestepped into the room, swinging around to face him, her gaze angry and challenging.

'Well?'

Letting his arms fall heavily to his sides, Brian expelled a resigned breath. 'Look, I'm dead sorry about not making it to Yorkshire. I didn't get the chance to let you know. I see you got my surprise prezzies, though,' he went on with an amiable smile, nodding to the sideboard where some of the flowers were displayed in a tall, cut-glass water jug. 'I said for them to be delivered the night you got back from visiting your mam.'

'Thank you,' she responded politely, putting a yard or so more distance between them and moving across the room to the fireplace. 'They arrived when I came home from Hathersedge's. Just after I'd been told you were given the sack for not showing up!'

'Ah, that!' He grimaced, rubbing his chin with the palm of his hand and going on contritely: 'I never got around to telling them. There just wasn't time, queen! Everything kicked off so fast. Well, you know that, of course.'

'No, Brian. That's where you're wrong. I *don't* know! I don't know anything at all!' she cried angrily. 'Where you've been! What you've been doing! Nothing! Have you any idea how worried I've been? About — about all sorts of things!'

'I am so, so sorry, queen,' he murmured humbly, gazing across at her from lowered eyes. 'It couldn't be helped. You'll understand, when we've had a chance to talk.'

Ellen squared her shoulders and marched past him to the door. Hot tears were stinging behind her eyes and she turned to face Brian stonily before they spilled. 'You — you let me and my family down with as little thought as you gave Hathersedge's! Please just go.'

'Hey, queen! Don't be so hasty!' He reached out in a helpless gesture. 'You know what I'm like! Sometimes I get carried away and go off doing things without thinking it out properly. I'm not surprised you're angry at me, but I am truly sorry.

'Won't you let me explain everything from the beginning?' he implored. 'I love you, Nellie! Just listen to me, please!'

She met his warm brown eyes, saw his earnest expression, and felt her resistance and resentment crumbling.

Fair was fair, after all. It was only right she heard him out. Besides, Ellen didn't want to lose him. She loved him.

'Very well.' She sat primly on one of the easy chairs.

With a sigh of relief, Brian sat across from her, leaning forward, elbows on his knees, his hands linked. 'I was at my digs, ready to go to the station, when Rodge turned up. Said he was sailing with the next tide and he needed a crew. Urgent.

'He was skippering a little cruise for a party of businessmen and the bloke he'd signed on as mate cried off at the last minute — '

'So, at the drop of a hat, you abandoned all your own plans and went off on some jolly with your old shipmate!'

'It wasn't like that, Nellie! Honestly, it wasn't. Roger's a good bloke and he was in a right bind. He couldn't man the boat single-handed. He's trying to build up some freelance work and he didn't want to lose this job, or fall out with the businessmen aboard. A couple of them are pretty important.

'I'm Rodge's only real friend in Liverpool so he came to me, begging for help. He was desperate, Nellie. We had to sail within the hour. By the time I got to thinking, we were aboard and it was all too late and I just hoped you'd gone on ahead without me.'

'I can understand your missing the train,' she commented wearily. 'But I've waited and worried about you for more than a whole week! Have you the slightest idea what that's been like?'

'There was no way I could get in touch,' he returned. 'I remember you saying your mam's shop doesn't have a telephone. The next best thing I could do was send the flowers and a message for when you got back to Liverpool.'

'*Letters*, Brian!' she exclaimed in exasperation. 'If you'd even scribbled a single line, I could have had that letter on Saturday morning, and wouldn't have spent the rest of the week imagining all sorts of horrible things!'

He shrugged. 'I never thought of writing a letter. Sorry. Anyhow, I don't know the address of your mam's shop.

'But listen — ' Reaching across, Brian laced Ellen's fingers with his own. ' — that trip with Rodge may turn out to be the opportunity of a lifetime!'

'Why is that?' she asked distractedly, her skin tingling at the touch of his hand.

'Once we got out to sea and I had a chance to size things up, I realised I might be on to a good thing.'

'You mean crewing boats for people? Like Roger does?'

He shook his head. 'I got talking to one of the businessmen aboard, a bloke called Jack McBride. Has ships here in town. We hit it off pretty well, and I got to thinking if I played my cards right, it might lead to something big. And there's a good chance it has.'

To Ellen's astonishment, he rose to leave.

'Is that all?'

'Nothing's definite yet, and I want to

wait until it's rock-solid before I tell you,' he answered blithely. 'Can I come round for dinner on Sunday?'

'I suppose so.'

'Great! Actually I've already promised Mrs Cummings I'll tidy up the garden and fix that bit of broken fence,' he grinned, bending to kiss her. 'After we've had our dinner, you and me'll go out somewhere quiet. If this business with Jack McBride pans out, there's going to be no looking back for us, Nellie!'

★   ★   ★

'It's a surprise,' Brian insisted on Sunday afternoon when they were walking from Laburnum Avenue. 'I'm not giving you any clues.'

'It's not Christie Park,' considered Ellen as they crossed to the bus stop. 'That's in the other direction.'

'You'll find out where we're going soon enough,' he replied when a bus appeared. 'I'm glad you put your warm coat and hat on, though!'

Ellen was dumbfounded when the bus finally stopped at the Pier Head and they alighted on the cold, blustery waterfront. Whipped by an offshore wind, the incoming tide was high and rough, cutting up into murky brown furrows and crashing against the hulls of vessels moored along the dockside.

'The Pier Head?' she enquired, raising her voice to be heard above the wind and tide. 'What are we doing here?'

'Want to show you something.' Putting an arm about her shoulders, Brian turned her around so they were facing the prestigious Victorian buildings dominating the waterfront. 'See that doorway over there? That's Jack McBride's office.'

'The businessman you met on that trip with Roger?'

Brian nodded. 'McBride's had ships in Liverpool since the twenties. It's a small line, but before the war they ran regular routes to Australia and Singapore. As well as short runs across to Ireland and the Isle of Man. Cargo, not passengers.

'Since the war, the company's gradually been picking up its old routes, and McBride's expanding,' finished Brian, grinning all over his face. 'He's spending more time away from Liverpool now, so he was looking for somebody to work in the office here — and I got the job!'

'You've another job already?' exclaimed Ellen in delight. 'That's wonderful!'

'Isn't it just! I told you McBride and me hit it off on the cruise. He saw the way I worked and we got talking, Saw eye-to-eye about things, y'know,' related Brian proudly. 'He mentioned there might be a job going when we got back to Liverpool. I went to see him in his office, and that was that — end of story!'

'Will you be going back to sea?' she asked in sudden consternation.

He shrugged. 'I suppose sometimes I might go out on the boats to check things, but my job's here in the office.

'Jack McBride's not getting any younger, and my guess is he's looking for a right-hand man he can trust. I intend to be that man, queen. I know boats. I know seamen. I know sailing. There's going to be no stopping me now!' Brian caught her up into his arms, his warm brown eyes laughing down into hers. 'Haven't you got anything to say? It's not like you to be stuck for words!'

'I can't believe it!' she murmured breathlessly, her eyes shining. 'It's . . . amazing!'

He drew in a deep breath, suddenly serious.

'I would've liked us to be wed as soon as I got out of the Navy, but I had nothing to offer you then. It's different now.'

Tenderly cupping Ellen's face, Brian touched her lips with a lingering kiss. 'We've waited long enough, Nellie — let's get married!'

# 7

The next few weeks flew by in a flurry of letters between Whinforth and Liverpool, wedding plans, and Brian's settling into his new post at Jack McBride's waterfront office.

For Ellen at Hathersedge's, the gossip and scandal surrounding his ignoble departure from the department store had finally petered out and life there was more or less back to normal. At lunchtimes, she and Hilary usually met up, but today Ellen was seeing Brian. He'd asked her to meet him outside Hathersedge's and she spotted him at once, propping up the bus pole with one shoulder and waving wildly to attract her attention.

'What's the surprise this time?' she asked, longing for more than the quick kiss he'd bestowed upon her cheek. 'Which bus today?'

With that, he stepped out into the busy street with an extravagant flourish of his arm and flagged down a taxi cab. 'Travelling in style today, queen! We're going somewhere special!'

The taxi cab climbed up through the town, passing the redbrick university and scholastic libraries, elegant Victorian squares and crescents, before turning into a tree-lined terrace of neat houses.

Paying off the taxi driver and tipping generously, Brian was so pleased he looked fit to burst as he ushered Ellen towards four stone steps leading up to a tall front door.

'What do you reckon?' he asked, his lips close to her ear. 'Fancy this as our first home?'

'Here?' she echoed in disbelief, twisting around to face him. 'We can't afford somewhere like this!'

'We can,' he retorted confidently. 'It's been empty a long while and the landlord hasn't done anything to it since before the war, so the rent's reasonable. We'll soon fix it up and then as soon as we've a deposit put by, we'll buy our own house. Renting's a mug's game. Owning your own property is the thing to do.'

'You have it all worked out, don't you?' she laughed, taking in the house and its pleasing surroundings.

'Pretty much!' He took keys from his pocket and jingled them. 'Would the future Mrs Kennedy care to enter this desirable abode?'

'It's beautiful!' she breathed, stepping into a high-ceilinged hallway with a staircase directly ahead and several doors opening off to the right, with another at the far end opposite the front door.

'The landlord's never bothered putting electricity in, but the gas is switched on,' explained Brian, opening a box of matches. 'I'll just light a couple of the lamps . . . There!'

Ellen ventured deeper into the house, wandering through the first door into a well-proportioned room with a large sash window. 'Look, it has shutters! And oh, what a lovely old fireplace — ' she began, as Brian took her into his arms, kissing her long and very slowly.

From necessity, it was a whirlwind tour of the house. Punctuality was a habit for Ellen and she was always back from lunch promptly. As for Brian, he'd soon observed his new boss didn't suffer fools or tardiness gladly, so he was making certain he didn't fall from favour by being late.

'If you don't like this house,' he commented, locking the front door behind them, 'I've spotted a few other possibles.'

'Like it? *I love it!*' cried Ellen, hugging his arm as they strode towards the main road in the hope of catching a taxi down into town. 'And you're right about the spare rooms upstairs, it would be wonderful to have Ma and Jeanette staying with us for our first Christmas in our very own home!

'Although I don't see how they'd be able to get away,' she went on practically. 'Even when Dad was alive, we could never go away for holidays, or even days out all together. Someone always had to stay behind and mind the shop.'

Brian shrugged. 'These things just need a bit of organising. I'm sure your mam could get somebody to hold the fort for a few days. It's only a paper shop, after all. Not much can go wrong, can it?'

However, Ellen's thoughts were already moving ahead on cautious lines.

'Before we take on the house, are you absolutely sure about this job at McBride's?'

'I'm doing it, aren't I?'

'Yes, for now. But what about the years ahead?' she persisted. 'Is working in the shipping office what you want to do? Won't you miss the adventure of the sea?'

'When I was in the Navy, the sea kept us apart. After we're married, I want to be with you all the time, Nellie,' he answered. 'I want to come home from McBride's every night and know you're in our house waiting for me — if that's alright with you!'

⋆　⋆　⋆

They fell into the habit of spending every weekend and most evenings cleaning and scraping, sanding, painting and papering at their new house. They were concentrating upon the front room and the kitchen, before tackling the other rooms.

'It looks so nice, now it's nearly finished,' commented Ellen in satisfaction, sitting on the white-spattered floorboards of the front room and digging a Thermos flask from her bag. 'I can't wait to put up curtains and get the lino and furniture in!'

Brian took a long draw on his tea. 'Why don't you and Hilary go out and buy what we need?'

'Don't you want to come with me?' she queried, disappointed. 'I was looking forward to our choosing everything together!'

91

'What time do I have for trailing round shops?' he asked mildly. 'I'm working all hours at the office!'

'I know.' She nodded with a smile. 'Hilary and I will make a start during our lunch hour tomorrow. She was only saying the other day she'd seen some nice curtaining material.'

'Are you sure you don't mind not having the wedding back in Yorkshire?' began Brian after a moment. 'It just seemed easier to get hitched here because I can't take time off from McBride's, but I suppose if you really — '

Ellen knelt beside him, wrapping her arms about him. 'I'm happy getting married right here!'

'Sure?'

'Positive! And the registry office is near enough for us to bring our guests back home with us,' she went on. 'So we can have a housewarming party as well as a wedding breakfast!'

'That's a great idea, queen!' exclaimed Brian enthusiastically. 'I'll ask Nick to sort out the eats. He's started doing a bit of catering now, you know.'

'I believe so. Hilary was telling me about it. She goes into his bakery every day. The insurance company has hired him to provide refreshments for a retirement party.'

'Nick reckons the catering side is building up nicely,' commented Brian. 'He's already offered to make the cake for us, so that'll be all the food done.'

'Brian, I know this is a sore subject for you, but what about your family?' she began carefully. 'A wedding is the perfect opportunity for people to forgive and forget and make up their differences.'

'You mean well, but frankly, queen, you haven't a clue what you're talking about,' he responded tersely. 'For my side of the guests, I'm inviting the McBride's, a few of the blokes from the shipping office and any old shipmates who are in town. Nobody else. Okay?'

'No! No, it isn't okay,' she returned passionately. 'From what little you've told me, you have parents and a brother. You're not being fair to them, Brian! Cutting them out like this. Not even giving them the chance to let bygones be bygones and come to your wedding!'

'Like I told you, Nellie, I've no family,' he snapped, glowering at her. 'I walked out when I was a lad. I haven't heard or set eyes on any of them since.

'It's best left that way, Nellie,' concluded Brian vehemently. 'So just forget it — understand?'

★ ★ ★

' ... are you pleased with the arrangements so far?' Hilary was asking, when the friends were at the house during their lunch-hour, hanging curtains in the big front room.

'Oh, yes!' replied Ellen enthusiastically. The registry office was booked, the catering arranged with Brian's friend Nick, and thanks to Hilary's flair and skill with needle and thread, Ellen's wedding outfit finished and hanging in her wardrobe. 'Everything's going along wonderfully smoothly. And thanks so much for all you're doing to help, Hilary!'

'I'm enjoying every minute, Nell,' she replied sincerely, stepping into the centre of the room to admire their handiwork. 'It's very satisfying making ready a new home. Bernard and I never did, of course. We had a room at his parents' for the short while we were married, but finding a house and turning it into our home is something I would've loved us to do together.'

Ellen squeezed her friend's arm affectionately. 'You'll do it one day, Hilary! There's a kind and loving man somewhere out there for you, you just wait and see!'

'Well unless I bump into him between here and Dean Street, I'd better get back to my desk at the insurance company!' laughed the older woman, gathering up her coat, hat and handbag. 'I hope you and Brian have a smashing evening — see you at home later!'

Before returning to Hathersedge's that afternoon, Ellen stowed groceries in the pantry and stacked pots, pans and cutlery onto the kitchen shelves, because after work she was coming back to the house to cook the very first meal she and Brian would share in their new home.

The front room was complete. With the linoleum down and a thick oval carpet in the centre, the room was comfortably furnished with a dining table and chairs, plus a three-piece-suite purchased from the local auction rooms. The kitchen was also finished and functioning. Most of the upstairs still needed attention, but the house was ready for them to move into after they married, and already felt like home.

That evening, she caught the bus from town and alighted at the corner of the terrace. Letting herself into the house, Ellen hummed softly as she bustled about lighting the gas lamps, closing the curtains against the wet evening and putting a match to the fire she'd built earlier.

She prepared a traditional hotpot that wouldn't spoil if Brian was kept late at the shipping office, as he so often was these days. However, to Ellen's delight, he arrived home promptly. She was pouring evaporated milk into a pretty jug to accompany the marmalade pudding when she heard the front door and ran to greet him.

★   ★   ★

'That was great, Nellie!' he sighed after they'd eaten, sinking into the settee and drawing her down beside him. 'The first meal you've ever cooked for me — I'll remember this evening for the rest of my life!'

'What a lovely thing to say!'

'This is just the start,' he said against the softness of her hair. 'We've got the rest of our lives together to look forward to.'

Ellen snuggled closer, utterly content. The wet night and crowded city outside seemed a world away.

Brian pulled her to him, and they remained curled up together on the settee, watching the flickering fire. Ellen may even have drifted into sleep when a gentle tapping upon the tall front door stirred her.

'Brian,' she murmured, pushing herself up onto one elbow. 'There's somebody knocking on the door!'

'That's what it's there for!' he grinned, easing himself away from her and crossing the room. 'Our first caller! Wonder who it is?'

Then he darted back, grasping Ellen's hand and hauling her to her feet. 'Come on, let's answer it together!'

Giggling, and with arms entwined, they stumbled down the hallway and Brian drew open the heavy door.

'Hilary!'

She was standing on the broad stone step, her face blanched to ghostly whiteness in the wavering beam shed by the nearby streetlight. Rain was pouring in rivulets from her mackintosh, hair and face, and she was hatless, seemingly oblivious to the inclement weather.

'Get yourself inside, girl!' Brian exclaimed, catching hold of her arm. 'Here, take your coat off — '

Hilary shook her head, her eyes troubled as she fished into the patch pocket of her mackintosh and withdrew a damp, crumpled envelope.

'This telegram came for you, Nell,' she murmured. 'I brought it straight here.'

Ellen was suddenly weak at the knees. Beneath the warm glow of the flickering gas lamps, she tore open the envelope, and with trembling fingers unfolded the single sheet of flimsy paper.

# 8

*Ma ill. Please come home. Jeanette.*

'It doesn't say what's wrong.' mumbled
Ellen, pushing the telegram into Brian's
hands. 'Ma must be really bad! Jeanette
wouldn't send a telegram — '

'This is guaranteed to frighten the
life out of anybody!' exclaimed Brian in
annoyance, scanning the short message.
'What was that sister of yours thinking
about? She could at least have given
you some idea what's happened!'

'I daresay Jeanette was anxious when
she sent it,' put in Hilary gently.

'Ma didn't look herself when we were
there for her birthday, did she, Hil?'
muttered Ellen, distractedly looking around
for her coat and handbag. 'It must be
really serious for Jeanette to send for me!'

'Is there any way you can get in touch
with Jeanette?' enquired Hilary practically. 'Any friends or neighbours who

have a telephone and could go to the shop and fetch her to speak to you?'

'That's a good idea,' agreed Brian. 'We can go down the square to the phone box and — '

'There's no time.' Ellen shook her head decisively. 'While we're doing that, I could be on my way home.'

'All I'm saying is,' persisted Brian. 'if you speak to Jeanette, she can put your mind at rest and stop you thinking the worst!'

'I just need to catch the next train and get to Whinforth straight away!' blurted Ellen desperately, raising huge, scared eyes to his. 'Will you come with me?'

'I can't, queen,' he answered quickly. Apologetically. Clasping both her hands into his. 'I'm sorry. I daren't. Not with this new job. McBride doesn't have any truck with people who don't pull their weight.'

'I'll come,' Hilary said softly, hoping against hope the last train to Yorkshire hadn't already departed. 'We'll go straight to the station.'

'You can't take more time off, Hilary! 'Specially without asking first,' replied Ellen sensibly. 'I'll be fine on my own. I just wish Whinforth wasn't so far away! It takes so long to get there!'

'Hang on a minute, Nellie — ' Brian reached out as Ellen pulled on her coat. 'You don't even know if there's another train tonight!'

But Ellen was already sweeping past him towards the front door. 'The sooner I get to the station, the sooner I'll find out — I have to get home!'

Hastily dousing the fire and turning off the gas, Brian strode after her, dragging on his own coat and shutting the tall front door securely behind them.

Squinting through the fine, driving rain, Brian scanned the traffic streaming along the main road, cursing softly under his breath. 'Why isn't there ever a taxi when you need one?'

They started down into the town towards the train station, marching as fast as their feet would carry them along the rain-soaked flagstones.

'Please God I haven't missed the last train!' prayed Ellen silently when finally they reached the station, and she broke away, running ahead towards the ticket office windows.

'Slow down! We've got time!' Brian caught up with her, pointing up to the departure board. 'Last train leaves in twelve minutes. You and Hilary sit yourselves down on the bench over there while I get your ticket.'

'No, Brian,' interrupted Hilary, meeting his gaze meaningfully. 'You stay with Nell. I'll sort out the ticket.'

'Er, right. Thanks.' He rubbed his chin awkwardly, taking Ellen's arm and guiding her over to the bench. 'I'm sorry I can't come with you, queen. I would if I could. You do know that, don't you?'

She nodded, turning anguished eyes upon him. 'She wasn't well when I saw her last, Brian. What if — what if Ma's . . . ' She couldn't frame the words; just stared up at him.

'Hey, we'll have none of that sort of talk!' he chided, taking her cold, wet hands. 'Your mam's going to be fine. Jeanette's likely had a bit of a fright and wants her big sister to come home. Can't blame her for that, can we?'

'Hold me,' mumbled Ellen. 'Hold me tight!'

He drew her to him, and Ellen surrendered into the comfort of his closeness and the security of his arms wrapped around her as she closed her eyes tight, burrowing her face into the coarse weave of his overcoat.

'Nell?' Hilary spoke very softly and Ellen raised her head, roughly scrubbing dry her face with the back of her hand. 'Nell, here's your ticket. Don't trouble about anything here. I'll let Hathersedge's know what's happened, and if you need to get in touch urgently, telephone me at the insurance office. I've written down the number.' She pressed a slip of paper together with the train ticket into Ellen's hands.

'They won't object to my receiving a personal call, not in the circumstances.

'There's only a few minutes until your train leaves. I'll wait here while Brian sees you aboard.' Hilary stepped forward, hugging her friend. 'God bless, Nell. Be sure to give your mum and Jeanette my love. If you need anything — anything at all — you need only ask.'

Unable to speak, Ellen nodded fiercely and let Brian lead her towards the smoky platform where the short train was noisily getting up steam for departure. Pausing at the ticket barrier, Ellen waved to Hilary. Wondering when, and under what circumstances, they would meet again.

'There's not many people aboard,' Brian was saying, steering her clear of the sparks spitting and flying as the fireman stoked the engine. 'You'll have your pick of seats.'

Brian chose an empty compartment, and in those few remaining minutes before parting, Ellen clung to him wordlessly, wishing with all her heart he could come with her and she didn't have to make the journey alone.

Then he was gently pushing her from him. The guard was striding along the platform, slamming doors, shouting to a few tardy passengers racing through the barrier. The whistle shrieked.

'I have to go.' Brian breathed, stroking her hair. 'Everything'll be alright, queen. You'll see.'

A last kiss, and Brian was gone.

Off the train and onto the platform as the train screeched and strained and began to chug slowly away. Ellen pushed down the window and leaned out over the door, watching him standing there as the distance separating them steadily increased. Further away still, and barely visible through the steam, she spotted Hilary at the ticket barrier, her hand raised in farewell.

Ellen waved to them both, her eyes dry now but stinging from the acrid smoke. Gradually, it thickened into a dense, smut-streaked fog engulfing the platform until Brian and Hilary were lost from Ellen's sight. The train curved out of the station and she was on her way to Yorkshire.

Pushing up the window, Ellen turned and walked unsteadily along the rocking corridor to the empty compartment. Sitting beside the window, she stared out into the blackness, willing the slow nighttrain to go faster as the miles dividing her from her mother and home yawned endlessly before her.

She wasn't clad for travelling, and was soon chilled to the bone in her damp clothing and shoes. Ellen scarcely noticed the discomfort. She was shivering with anxiety as much as cold; huddled stiffly, her arms wrapped about herself.

Ma had worked hard all her life. She wasn't strong. How seriously ill was she? Fear and sorrow shrouded Ellen during those long desolate hours, while the miles slowly ground away beneath the rattling wheels and she fought to push away the one thought that would not be shut out —

What if Ellen was already too late?

* * *

The seasons were turning. It was past six o'clock when Ellen arrived in Whinforth, but whereas just weeks earlier the day would already have been light and warm, upon this morning the darkness of night clung and there was an unmistakably autumnal chill in the air, made all the keener by the north-easterly gusting down from the Dow Hills. The local buses were already running, and Ellen had only to wait a few minutes at the Great War memorial before the bus for Market Street juddered to a halt and she hauled herself aboard.

Stepping down onto the flagstones just a short way from the Butterworths' corner shop, Ellen ran the rest of the way home. Would Jeanette be there, sitting up with Ma? Would Ma be at home? No, at the Infirmary, surely —

The shop came into plain sight and Ellen was knocked sick to her stomach. It was in total darkness. There was no sign of life. The stout door with its two narrow glass panes was closed. That morning's delivery of newspapers and magazines remained stacked in the doorway. A heap of coins lay in the corner. The Butterworths' regular customers had dug their own papers from the pile and left payment tucked behind the stack.

Ellen absorbed it all in a quick glance, already darting down the ginnel and bursting through the back door into the whitewashed yard. Still no lights! In mounting panic, she peered up at the windows. The curtains were all wide open. Everywhere was blackness. Nobody was home. Dear Lord, was she too late —

Fumbling for her key, Ellen heard a desperate cry from within the house and the kitchen door wrenched open.

'Nellie! Oh, Nell — ' A slender girl with a mop of tousled golden curls cannoned from the darkness and flung herself at Ellen. 'I've been waiting hours — I thought you'd *never* come!'

'Ma?' mumbled Ellen thickly, ready to hear the worst. 'Ma, is she — '

'She's still alive, but only just!' blurted Jeanette, her voice trembling. 'It's serious, Nellie. Ma's really bad. They took her away. They've put her on Urgent Note. They sent me home. I've been sitting here all night!'

'We're together now, Jenny,' soothed Ellen, sending up a silent prayer of thanks. That the Infirmary had placed their mother on Urgent Note, however, scared her. Only seriously ill patients whose lives were in danger were treated with such intensive care. She hugged her young sister's bowed shoulders as they went indoors. 'I know you must be tired, but will you fetch your coat? We'll go straight up to the Infirmary. I want to see Ma.'

'You can't!' cried Jeanette. 'They won't let us see her. She's unconscious. I wanted to stay at the Infirmary last night, but they wouldn't let me. They said not to come back until later this morning after Doctor Irwin's done his rounds.'

Ellen hesitated, trying to think clearly. Her every instinct was to rush to the hospital. Even if they couldn't be at Ma's bedside, at least they would be nearby. On the other hand, they could hardly turn up against doctors' orders. 'Very well. It is still very early. We'll wait a while.'

She moved across to the sink and began filling the kettle. Glancing around, Ellen was struck by the chill dankness of the usually bright, cheery kitchen. The grate was heaped with grey, dead ashes and the stove cold and silent. 'I'll make breakfast while you tell me exactly what happened.'

'I can't face food.' Jeanette dropped to her knees at the hearth and set to shovelling the ashes. 'I'm not hungry.'

'Nor am I, but we should try to eat something.' answered Ellen, turning on lights and fetching milk and bread from the pantry. 'You said Ma was unconscious, Jen. What's the matter with her?'

'I don't know! The nurses wouldn't tell me anything!' wailed Jeanette,

111

twisting around on her knees to look up at her elder sister. 'All they'd say was that the doctors were examining Ma and they'd know more this morning.'

'I suppose that makes sense. They may need time to find out what's wrong,' frowned Ellen, stirring coarse oatmeal into a pan of creamy milk. 'Has Ma been poorly? Hilary and I thought she looked a bit tired and peaky when we came home for her birthday.'

'She's had a bad chest for a couple of weeks, and this awful damp weather always makes it worse,' replied Jeanette bleakly. 'Ma didn't want to bother Doctor Irwin, so I got her a bottle from the chemist. She wouldn't stay in bed, or even let me take her turn doing the morning papers. She just kept getting up as usual.'

'That's Ma all over!' declared Ellen softly, running her hand across Dorothy's freshly-laundered apron, folded neatly on the corner of the dresser. 'Was she taken ill when she was out?'

'No, she was here! In the shop.'

Jeanette paused, staring at her grimy hands. 'It was quiet after the teatime rush, so I went to the library to change our books while Ma started getting ready to close up.

'When I got back an hour or so later, the shop was shut and Ma was gone and Mrs Heggie was here waiting for me!' she gulped, her huge blue eyes wide and dry. 'She'd called in for young Robbie's *Rainbow* and some pear drops. Nobody was behind the counter so she waited a bit. Then she called, 'Shop!' When nobody answered, she leaned over the counter to shout through to the back, and . . . and then she saw Ma lying on the floor!'

'Had she had a fall?'

Jeanette shook her head. 'She'd collapsed, I think. Mrs Heggie said Ma was unconscious and burning up. She went next door and Mrs Clough sent young Billy to fetch Doctor Irwin.

'When I got back from the library the ambulance was disappearing up the hill! The light was flashing and everything!'

sobbed the girl, tears flowing freely now. 'I didn't see Ma, Nellie! I didn't even see her!'

Ellen went to the hearth, folding Jeanette into her arms and rocking her gently as she had when her sister was a small child. 'Doctor Irwin knows Ma well and he's a fine doctor. He'll be taking good care of her, Jen, and perhaps he'll let us see her this morning.'

Ellen rose, patting Jeanette's shoulder. 'While you finish lighting the fire, I'll fetch the papers in. After we've had a bite to eat and been to see Ma, we'll open the shop.'

'You're opening the shop?'

'We'll pin a note on the door saying we'll open later for a few hours.' Ellen was certain keeping busy would be best for both of them. Idleness offered far too much opportunity for brooding. 'Ma wouldn't want her regular customers to be turned away. She'll want us to keep the shop open. We can't let her down.'

'You're right,' agreed Jeanette, shovelling the cinders. Without looking up from the empty grate, she went on: 'The Infirmary will tell us if . . . if anything happens to Ma, won't they? I mean, they'd send a message? Or a policeman or somebody to tell us?

'They would let us know — wouldn't they?'

★ ★ ★

The Infirmary, with its uniform rows of small square windows, had been built as the parish workhouse, its buildings given over as a hospital around the turn of the century. Glancing up at the tall, smoke-blackened walls, Ellen thought the Infirmary looked every bit as grim and intimidating now as it must've done during its workhouse days. The lantern-jawed almoner directed the sisters to a narrow corridor, where they sat tense and stiff-backed upon one of the hard wooden benches lining the bare distempered and half-tiled walls.

At length, a ward sister rustled towards them and Ellen rose to politely enquire about Dorothy.

'Mrs Butterworth is very poorly.' responded the senior nurse briskly, her attention leaving the sisters as she turned on her heel. 'Doctor Irwin is presently doing his rounds. He will have a word with you afterwards. You may continue to wait here.'

'But what's *wrong* with Ma?' cried Jeanette, leaping to her feet and following the nurse. 'Please tell us! Is she going to be alright?'

'Doctor will speak to you after his rounds,' repeated the ward sister firmly as she strode along the corridor, her footsteps ringing on the bare wooden floor.

'This is awful, Nellie,' mumbled Jeanette brokenly, falling back onto the bench. 'Why won't they tell us what's wrong with Ma? She must be really bad, mustn't she?'

'We don't know that!' exclaimed Ellen, adding reassuringly: 'The nurse said Doctor Irwin will see us shortly. He'll explain everything to us, I'm sure. And Ma couldn't be in better hands, could she?'

The elderly physician had been the Butterworths' doctor for many years and had brought both sisters into the world. Ellen had great faith in him. She reached across and squeezed Jeanette's hand. 'Not long to wait now!'

The clock seemed not to move, however, and the following hour of waiting crawled by. Ellen sat quite still, gripping her handbag. Her gaze seldom straying from the doors into the ward further along the corridor.

At long last, she heard the soft burr of the elderly man's voice as double doors swung noiselessly open and Cecil Irwin emerged, followed by four fresh-faced young men who had accompanied him on his rounds. With a final few words to the recently qualified physicians, Doctor Irwin approached the sisters.

'Why don't we pop into the cubby-hole I call my office so we can have a talk, eh?' he suggested, shepherding them towards a tiny windowless room lined with tightly-packed shelves. Easing himself behind a small desk, Doctor Irwin indicated the two chairs before it. 'Sit yourselves down, girls.

'You've waited a long while for news and I'll not mince words. Your mum's very poorly. She has a high fever. It's her chest again, but much more serious than anything she's had before. The next seventy-two hours will be critical.'

A tiny, anguished yelp escaped Jeanette's full lips. 'Is Ma going to die?'

'We're doing everything we can for your mum, Jeanette. She's had a fairly comfortable night and her condition now appears stable. The diphtheria she suffered during childhood weakened her constitution considerably, and that is causing added complications. We've run some tests and when the results come back, they'll tell us a good deal more about your mum's illness. We'll be keeping her on Urgent Note for a while longer, of course.'

'But — ' began Ellen, so many questions still unanswered. However, the doctor had risen, indicating the interview was over, so she quickly asked, 'Is Ma in pain, Doctor Irwin? Can we at least see her? Let her know we're here with her?'

'Dorothy's not properly conscious, you understand. The fever causes her to be fitful,' responded Cecil Irwin carefully. 'But yes, you may look in on her. Just for a moment. Then if you'll take my advice, you'll go home and get some rest. There's nothing more you can do here.'

Ushering them from his office, he led them into a small, dimly-lit ward where three other gravely ill patients lay in high, narrow beds. For Jeanette's sake, Ellen had tried to steel herself; but nonetheless, she could not suppress a cry of shock.

Their mother looked very small and helpless, lying fretfully beneath starched white hospital linen. Her gaunt face was flushed and moist, her hollow eyes appeared to be working behind closed, waxy lids. Ellen felt Jeanette's hand grip her own so tightly, the fingernails dug painfully into her palm.

Ma was barely clinging on to life. She knew nothing of their presence, nor of anything happening around her.

★ ★ ★

'Poor Ma might've been lying here all alone for hours,' reflected Jeanette sorrowfully, gazing around the empty shop when the girls went in early that afternoon. A broken jar of humbugs and crushed packets of cigarettes lay strewn over the worn linoleum, where they'd been knocked when Dorothy had staggered and fallen. 'If Mrs Heggie hadn't come in when she did, Ma might've . . . might've . . .'

'Thank heavens Ada *did* come along!' interrupted Ellen gently. 'We must visit her. Thank her for everything she did.'

'Oh, Nellie — what are we going to

do without Ma!' cried Jeanette. 'What'll we do without her?'

'The best we can.' Ellen disappeared into the kitchen and returned with a dustpan and brush. 'We have to get ourselves organised, Jen. Doctor Irwin asked us not to visit Ma again today, so we'll open the shop for a couple of hours at teatime. From tomorrow, we'll open and do everything as usual.'

'How can we?' demanded Jeanette. 'With Ma ill like she is?'

'What else can we do?' reasoned Ellen, on her knees and sweeping up the broken glass and scattered sweets. 'It'll be ages before Ma's well enough to look after the shop herself. Meanwhile, we have to make sure she has a thriving little shop to come back to!

'Now, the kitchen fire's been lit so there should be plenty of hot water. Why don't you have a nice relaxing bath and then get yourself into bed? You'll feel better once you've had some sleep.'

The younger woman hovered in the

curtained doorway separating shop from house. 'What about you, Nellie? You must be worn out. You've been up all night, too.'

Ellen shook her head. 'I'd sooner keep going. Besides, I need to go out and telephone Brian and Hilary.'

★   ★   ★

It was going to be another cold night, so while Jeanette took her bath, Ellen lit fires in both their bedrooms and tucked a stone hot water bottle into her sister's bed. Taking a handful of small coins from the cash drawer, she hurried from the shop, turning along Cross Street towards the Post Office and the telephone box outside. She was longing for the comfort of being close to Brian, albeit only over the telephone wires. It already seemed such a long while since they'd been together.

'Sorry, miss.' The voice of McBride's junior clerk crackled across the distance. 'Mr Kennedy's not in the office.

He's gone down to the docks to meet one of our ships.'

Ellen left a brief message, adding that she would telephone again that evening, certain Brian would be working late.

She was more fortunate in reaching Hilary. Mindful of the insurance company's disapproval of employees receiving personal calls, the friends spoke only long enough for Ellen to explain what had happened and promise to write. Hurrying back to the shop, Ellen opened up for the evening papers and teatime rush. When she thankfully closed the door behind the last customer and switched off the light, she went upstairs and peeped in at Jeanette's bedroom. She was still sleeping soundly. Creeping from the room, Ellen went downstairs. Glancing at her wristwatch and putting on her coat, she slipped out and made for the telephone box.

The call to the shipping office was at long last connected, and Brian came to the telephone.

'Hello, love!' he exclaimed briskly.

'Sorry I missed you earlier on. There was a problem with one of our ships coming in, and the harbourmaster sent word for me to go down and sort it out.'

Ellen closed her eyes tightly, clutching the telephone with both hands, cherishing even this tenuous nearness. 'Oh, Brian — I wish you were here!'

Suddenly, her resolve to be strong crumbled, and Ellen yearned to be wrapped in the warmth of his arms.

'It's awful! Ma's very ill! I don't think they're sure what's really wrong yet. She's got a terrible fever and she hasn't even woken up yet. She's been poorly with her chest before, but this is different. They've got her on Urgent Note. Doctor Irwin says the next seventy-two hours will be critical, but Brian, what if — '

'Your mam's going to get better, Nellie,' he interrupted firmly, his deep voice confident and reassuring. 'It's amazing what doctors can do these days, so don't you go worrying yourself sick, you hear me?'

'That's what Dr Irwin said.'

'He's right and all,' opined Brian positively. 'So, have you any idea when you're coming home?'

'Home?' she echoed absently. 'Oh, coming back to Liverpool . . . I hadn't even thought about it!'

'No. No, of course you haven't, queen,' he murmured apologetically. 'It's just me being selfish. I miss you such a lot already, and you haven't been away a day yet!'

'If only you could get up here!' she blurted, her voice shaky. 'It's awful without Ma. We only saw her for a few minutes and she didn't know we were there. I'm scared she's going to die, Brian! I'm so frightened!'

'I know you are, queen. But your mam'll make it, you'll see. Ah, I wish I could give you a big hug and a kiss!' he mumbled thickly. 'I'd be with you if I could, but I'm still the new boy at the office. I can't go asking McBride for time off.'

'I know, love,' she murmured sensibly. 'It can't be helped.'

'Anyhow, it probably makes more sense for me to stay here and get on with the house so it'll be ready when you come home,' he went on. 'Tell you what, why don't I go round to Mrs C's tonight and bring her and Hilary up to date with what's going on?'

'I'd be glad if you would. I have spoken to Hilary, but only for a moment.' She paused, loath to put down the telephone. 'I love you, Brian — I miss you terribly!'

★　★　★

Exhaustion was fast overtaking her, but resisting the longing to head homewards to her bed, Ellen made her way along Cross Street and up through the town towards the River Whin.

Once over the ancient drovers' bridge, the landscape opened out. The dark, deep waters of the Whin rushed alongside Ellen as she walked, while across the river the solid blackness of the Dow Hills rose up and melded into a starless sky. At her left side, the footpath curved away from the river and Ellen followed it round to Lane End House, where Ada Heggie kept house for the Munros.

Pushing open the gate, she hesitated a fraction before veering away from the front door and starting around the edge of the garden towards the side entrance. However, she'd taken no more than a few paces when she heard a quiet tap on the window and turned to see Mr Munro drawing aside the heavy velvet curtains and beckoning her to wait.

A moment later, he was opening the front door and light spilled out into the chill evening.

'Miss Butterworth?' He removed his spectacles as he spoke, the evening newspaper tucked beneath one arm, and extended his hand towards her. 'I'm Alex Munro. A customer at your mother's shop. I was very sorry to hear she's been taken ill. Please, do come in.'

'Thank you, but . . . well, actually it was Mrs Heggie I came to see,' she explained hurriedly, remaining on the doorstep. 'It was she who found Ma and raised the alarm. I'd like to thank her, if I may?'

'Of course! Won't you come inside, Miss Butterworth?' he repeated, standing aside so she might pass through the vestibule into a broad, carpeted hallway. 'If you'd like to go into the sitting-room — just to your right there — I'll fetch Mrs Heggie. She's in the kitchen.'

'No, really!' put in Ellen hastily. 'I don't want to disturb your evening, Mr Munro. Besides, I'm sure Ada will be busy. If I might just go into the kitchen and have a word with her . . . ?'

'If you'd prefer, by all means.' He smiled politely down at her before turning along the hallway and adding, 'Miss Butterworth, would you be so kind as to give my regards to your sister? And needless to say, if I can be of any practical assistance during this worrying time, please do not hesitate to ask.'

Taken aback by his unexpected kindness, Ellen could only murmur her heartfelt thanks as she looked up into Alex Munro's grave face. He was a tall man, already greying at the temples, and there was a quality about his quiet, gracious manner that was somehow old-fashioned and rather reassuring.

'Mrs Heggie — ' He pushed open the kitchen door and looked in. 'Here's Miss Butterworth to see you!'

Ada Heggie turned around from the electric cooker in surprise, her plump face freezing.

'It's not bad news about your ma — ?'

'Not at all!' reassured Ellen hastily. 'She's very ill, but Doctor Irwin told us Ma's as comfortable as can be expected. Jeanette and I saw her for a few minutes but she didn't know we were there.'

'Poor soul! You've all been in my prayers, lass,' sighed Ada, bustling across the spotless kitchen and pulling out one of the chairs from the square table. 'Sit yourself down, Nellie. You look like you could do with a good cup of tea.'

Ellen hesitated, wondering if she should stay while Ada was working; however, when she glanced over her shoulder to see Alex Munro's reaction, she realised he'd unobtrusively left the two women to their conversation.

'If you're sure it'll be alright,' she answered, adding humbly: 'We'll never be able to thank you enough for what you did, Ada. You saved Ma's life.'

'Ah, away!' Ada clattered cups and saucers down onto the table. 'I only did what anyone would've. I was just about to make the children's cocoa. How about nice hot milky cocoa instead of tea, Nellie? It's a sight more nourishing, and you look sorely in need of a pick-me-up!'

'I do feel a bit worse for wear!' admitted Ellen with a small smile. 'Cocoa would be really nice.'

'Good lass!' beamed the elderly woman. 'How about a pikelet to go with it?'

'Only if you'll let me toast them — I'm a whiz with a toasting-fork!'

Presently, Ada set the children's

cocoa cups and plates with the first of the hot buttered pikelets onto a polished wooden tray. 'I'll just take this up to the bairns — won't be a tick!'

Ellen sat before the kitchen fire, the pikelets keeping warm in a covered basket beside her, wondering what was happening at the Infirmary and whether Dorothy was any better and resting easier. The warmth of the fire and the comfortable quietness of the house enveloped her, and Ellen's eyelids grew heavy until she knew she'd nod off if she didn't stir her stumps. Rising, she went to the sink and splashed cold water onto her hanky, pressing the pad against her tired eyes.

Returning to the fireside, she sat listening to the muted sounds of the family settling down for the night: Ada's heavy footsteps moving along the landing; the creak of floorboards from the children's room above; muffled commentary from a wireless programme drifting along the hallway from the sitting-room, where Alex Munro was listening to the news on the Home Service.

' — that's Peggy and little Robbie tucked up for the night!' declared Ada, bustling into the kitchen. 'Mrs Sheelagh — their ma, that is — she always made bedtime special for the bairns. Cocoa, toast, reading stories, singing to them, all sorts . . . Since she's been gone, we've tried to keep it up, but it's not the same.

'Don't take me wrong,' she went on hastily, easing herself into her chair and propping her slippered feet onto the fender. 'Mr Munro does his best — but he's such a scholarly sort of gentleman! Can't imagine him ever being a little lad.'

'I don't recall having met him before this evening,' remarked Ellen, sipping her cocoa. 'He seems very pleasant. Considerate.'

'He's a good man, right enough. Him and Sheelagh were a grand couple. Moved down here when Mr Munro joined that firm of solicitors in Church Mews,' reflected Ada, topping up their cocoa cups. 'I was just their daily at first, but by and by they asked me to move in as housekeeper, and I've been here ever since.

'I was a bit surprised to see your ma's shop open this afternoon when I passed on the bus,' she concluded. 'You'll be wanting to keep things ticking over, I daresay?'

Ellen nodded, stifling a yawn. 'We're hoping to open more or less as normal from tomorrow . . . It's such a busy little shop.'

'Always has been. Your ma and dad used to be behind that counter morning, noon and night. Never had a day closed. 'Course, you can't, not with a newsagent's,' reflected Ada, adding bluntly, 'Jeanette mentioned you were getting wed soon. What does your young man say to you leaving him all on his tod to come up here?'

Ellen considered, her weary mind not immediately grasping Ada's meaning. 'When I got the message Ma was ill, Brian was as shocked as I was. We went straight to the train station.'

'I meant about you moving back home to mind the shop,' persisted Ada, draining the cocoa jug. 'Jeanette can't do it on her own, can she? It needs two people to run that shop.'

Ada's remarks about Brian were mithering Ellen's mind during the long walk back to Market Street. While he'd been in the Navy, she'd been accustomed to their not being together. Somehow, however, this separation already felt very different.

Letting herself into the backyard, Ellen was surprised to see light flooding from the kitchen window; the instant she pushed open the door, she was enfolded by the mouth-watering aromas of spices, fruit and baking.

'My word,' exclaimed Ellen, smiling across to her sister, who was wearing Ma's apron. 'You've been busy!'

'I found some candied peel Ma bought when she was out shopping yesterday,' began Jeanette, brushing a smudge of flour from her plump cheek. 'I've put a brack in the oven for us, and

I'm using the rest to make cakes. Do you think it'd be alright if I gave one to Mrs Heggie, and the other to young Billy from next door? As a sort of thank-you for all they did to help Ma?'

'That's a smashing idea!' beamed Ellen, hanging up her coat. 'After I telephoned Brian, I went up to see Ada. She sends her regards to you and Ma.'

'I can't stop thinking what might've happened if Mrs Heggie hadn't found Ma when she did,' mumbled Jeanette, concentrating upon lining the cake tins. 'It's horrible without Ma here, isn't it? What'll we do if — '

'Ma's going to get well and come home to us,' interrupted Ellen, with far more confidence than she truly felt. 'It's just going to take a while until she's better, that's all.'

'Nell, I know you've got Brian and a good job and your whole life is in Liverpool now,' Jeanette began hesitantly, not raising her eyes. 'But I'm so afraid . . .

'You won't go away and leave me on my own — will you?'

# 9

The days settled into a busy routine of the sisters sharing the work in the shop and house, and spending as many hours as Doctor Irwin allowed at the Infirmary: sitting at Dorothy's bedside and talking to her, or chatting cheerfully to each other, in the hope their mother could somehow hear their voices and know they were both there with her.

' . . . you run that shop so efficiently, Jen,' Ellen was saying upon one such evening. It had been another hectic day; what with an endless stream of customers and the Christmas stock starting to come in, they'd been rushed off their feet since before six that morning. 'While I've been away, you've grown up and become a highly accomplished businesswoman!'

'Don't know about that!' giggled the younger woman, glancing affectionately at Dorothy. She was looking much stronger these days, but still lay motionless as though sleeping. 'What do you think, Ma?'

'Ma's very proud of you — just like I am.'

'I do love our little shop!' beamed Jeanette, pink and pleased at the compliment from her elder sister. 'I've always liked being in there. Even when Dad was still here, I'd make a nuisance of myself trying to serve customers and rearrange the sweetie shelves!'

'Looking back, I feel guilty about when you left school,' began Ellen after a moment. 'You did far better at grammar school than I did, but you didn't have the chance to go on to college. Dad had died and you went straight into the shop to help Ma. It wasn't fair.'

'Don't fret about it, Nellie!' replied Jeanette at once. 'I stayed an extra year at school because Ma and Dad wanted me to, but I couldn't wait to leave. I'd have hated to go away to secretarial college like you did. All I wanted was to start work, and nothing's better than a family business! You can't beat working for yourself.'

'You sound like somebody else I know!' chuckled Ellen, her fingers lightly stroking Dorothy's thin hand. 'Brian has a good job in a shipping office now, but his great ambition is to have his own business one day — although he hasn't decided yet what it will be!'

'Good for him — Brian sounds a man after my own heart!' declared Jeanette with a laugh. 'I can't wait to meet him — in his picture, he looks a real dreamboat! I'm green with envy.'

'What about your leading man from the amateur dramatics society?' enquired Ellen archly. 'He's smitten with you, my girl!'

'He is not! Stephen Phillips and I are just pals,' responded Jeanette firmly. 'We joined the Whinforth Players at the same time last year, and the Christmas production is going to be our very first play. Since we're both fairly new members, we're helping each other out.'

'If you say so,' agreed Ellen readily, adding more seriously: 'It's nice talking like this, Jen. I wish we'd done it more often.'

'We've never had much chance. I was only little when you left home to go to secretarial college, and whenever you're home for holidays there never seems time for nattering — '

Jeanette broke off, gripping Ellen's hand. Their mother had stirred slightly. Now she was still again. Then her lips moved. Her eyes flickered, then closed, the lids too heavy to open.

'Ma!' whispered Jeanette, dropping to her knees at the bedside. 'Ma, we're here! We're with you!'

'Nurse!' called Ellen quietly, hurrying to the end of the ward where the duty nurse was seated working in the light of a shaded lamp. 'Please come — I think my mother's waking up!'

Ellen was back at the bedside in a flash, just as Dorothy's head moved slowly on the white pillow. As though very, very tired and waking from the deepest sleep, she was struggling to open her eyes. Scarcely able to focus on the faces swimming blurrily above her, Dorothy's forehead creased.

'Jen . . . and Nellie?' she mumbled. 'Nellie lass, what are you doing here . . . ?'

*   ★   ★

'It doesn't seem right,' protested Jeanette when they were closing up the shop for the night. 'Me going off to rehearsals as though nothing's happened!'

'Ma's out of danger now, and she'd want you to go,' reasoned Ellen, turning off the lights. 'Besides, when we visit her tomorrow, I'm not going to be the one who tells her you bunked off!'

'I'm just not in the mood.'

'Come on, Jen, buck up!' she urged. 'Why don't we have a bite to eat and I'll get the bus with you? While you're rehearsing, I'll pop into the library and choose some mysteries for us to read to Ma now she's feeling a bit better.'

They caught the bus across town towards Victoria Road, where the Whinforth Players met and put on their productions in the school's assembly hall. Ellen rose from her seat to alight at the lending library, but Jeanette caught her sleeve.

'Why don't you come to rehearsals with me? You used to like drama at school.'

'I'm not a member. I can't just turn up and watch rehearsals!'

'Nobody'd mind. The Players are a friendly crowd,' persisted Jeanette. 'Please come, Nellie! We're reading through the script tonight and this is my very first speaking part. I'm really nervous.'

'So I'll feel a heel if I refuse and plump for a quiet evening browsing in the library!' laughed Ellen. 'Alright, you win! And does the dashing Stephen have a role in this play of yours?'

Jeanette blushed slightly. 'Yes. Stephen's helping build sets, too. We're a small group and everybody pitches in with everything.'

Both sisters had started their school lives at Victoria Road, and when Jeanette led the way inside, Ellen recognised the smell of books, chalk dust and floor polish.

'Is Miss Thwaite still headmistress?'

'She's ancient, but still here ruling the roost,' grinned Jeanette. 'She runs the Whinforth Players with a rod of iron, too!'

They went quietly into the assembly hall. It was unlit except for the stage at the far end, where several bright lamps were burning. Eunice Thwaite was centre stage, organising a couple of people carrying furniture. Rows of small wooden chairs were set out before the stage, where other members of the Players were conversing in low voices, poring over their scripts or drinking strong tea.

A tall man rose from a seat near the sisters, removing his spectacles and greeting them pleasantly. 'Hello, Jeanette. Good evening, Miss Butterworth.'

'Hello, Alex.' Jeanette smiled. 'This is my sis — oh, but you've already met Nellie, haven't you?'

'Indeed so.' Alex Munro inclined his head courteously, extending a hand toward the row of chairs. 'Please, take a seat. Proceedings haven't yet begun, so you haven't missed — '

He was interrupted by Eunice Thwaite breaking off from directing the furniture and stepping forward to the edge of the stage. Shielding her eyes, she peered over the footlights into the shadowy hall.

'Jeanette! Glad you could make it. How's Mother? Delighted to hear she's turned the corner! Long way still to go, of course.'

'I've brought my sister to watch our rehearsal, Miss Thwaite,' began Jeanette. 'Is that alright?'

'Absolutely! The more the merrier,' responded Eunice, squinting into the dimness. 'Ellen? Ellen Butterworth? Grand to see you again! Know you anywhere. You haven't changed at all. Except for the pigtails. I'll introduce you to our motley crew . . . '

Ellen was greeted warmly by the rest of the Players, and while Jeanette took her place on stage, she slipped off her coat and settled into the seat beside Alex Munro.

'Would you like tea?' he enquired. 'It's from an urn, but generally quite palatable!'

'That'd be nice, thanks,' she replied, continuing when Alex returned with two thick white cups and saucers. 'Which part are you playing, Mr Munro?'

He shook his head wryly. 'Couldn't act to save my life, I'm afraid. I do enjoy being involved, though — providing it's behind the scenes. Although occasionally, Eunice does persuade me to dress as a butler and carry a silver tray onto the stage!'

Ellen laughed, noting the animated faces and good-natured banter between the Players. 'I've never belonged to any societies. Not much of a joiner, I suppose. But this all looks very enjoyable!'

'It is. And performances of our plays help raise funds for the needy. Especially the old and sick, and those families who lost the breadwinner during the war,' commented Alex, his gaze moving from Ellen to the stage where the actors were rustling their scripts and preparing to read. 'It was my late wife, Sheelagh, who introduced me to amateur dramatics. She had a fine speaking voice and was an excellent needlewoman, so she was always in great demand! Are you familiar with this play, Miss Butterworth?'

She shook her head. 'Jeanette told me it's *Mystery at Greenfingers* by J.B. Priestley, but I hadn't even heard of it.'

'It's a mystery — well, lots of mysteries, really! — set in the nineteen-thirties at a hotel on the edge of the Yorkshire moors. The weather takes a turn for the worse, roads are impassable, telephone lines down and the hotel becomes snowbound,' he explained enthusiastically. 'It's an ambitious choice for the Players, but Eunice has every confidence in her cast.

Perhaps you'd like to borrow my copy of the script?'

Eunice called Alex Munro onto the stage to stand in for one of the cast who'd been delayed, and the read-through began. It was a little halting and unsure at first, but gradually everyone's nerves settled and the Players got into their stride.

The evening flew by, and in no time the Whinforth Players were packing up and tidying away the chairs and make-shift props. Ellen lent a hand, and she and Jeanette were about to leave when Stephen Phillips edged towards them, colour rising to his smooth cheeks.

'Are you coming for a coffee, Jeanette?'

'Don't think so, Stephen. Not tonight.'

'Nonsense! You must come!'

Eunice had pricked up her ears and was advancing upon them. 'And you'll join us too, won't you, Ellen? We round off our evenings by repairing for refreshment to the coffee-house across the road.'

Ellen was about to decline, then glimpsed a certain wistfulness in her sister's eyes and hesitated.

'Do join us, Miss Butterworth,' put in Alex Munro quietly, switching off the lights as the last of the group filed from the hall and started along the corridor. 'You're most welcome.'

'A new face is always welcome,' grunted an elderly man with side-whiskers. 'We've too many old 'uns!'

The coffee-house was tucked between the bespoke tailor and a greengrocery. The proprietor stayed open late especially to accommodate the Whinforth Players, and the establishment was empty until they descended upon it, gathering around the small tables, drinking coffee and munching toasted teacakes. One of the Players picked up a guitar and began strumming *Bésame Mucho*; a few others joined in with the lyrics, singing softly.

It was a convivial atmosphere and Ellen was content to sit back, sip her coffee and listen. Occasionally, she glanced over to a corner table where Jeanette was happily chatting with Stephen and three other young friends.

Eunice Thwaite squeezed into the chair next to Ellen, stirring her from her reverie.

'Mind if I perch? I'm glad you're back in town, and I daresay you're going to stay a while,' began the headmistress amiably. 'I recall, during your schooldays you were adept at drawing and crafts. If you have any time to spare, extra pairs of hands are ever welcome in the Whinforth Players — ah, must go! Somebody's hailing me! Hope to see you at our next meeting, Ellen. We'll certainly find something useful for you to do!'

It was late when the Players began drifting away from the coffee-house, bidding each other cheerful farewells.

'Goodnight, Jeanette.' Alex Munro paused, holding the door for them. 'I'm very glad you were able to join us, Miss Butterworth. I hope you've had a pleasant evening and will perhaps find time to come again. Please do pass on my family's and Mrs Heggie's warmest regards to your mother.'

'Alex is really quite nice once you get to know him,' whispered Jeanette, stifling a giggle as the lawyer strode away along the dark street. 'But gee whiz, he's such a dry old stick, and frightfully stuffy!'

'Don't be unkind!' admonished Ellen mildly. 'Mr Munro's just chivalrous and well-mannered. A proper gentleman. And he's not so old, my girl!'

'You're joking!' grimaced Jeanette, slipping her arm through Ellen's. 'He must be thirty-five if he's a day!'

★   ★   ★

Dorothy was over the worst, but Doctor Irwin had not minced words when explaining the consequences of her illness to Ellen and Jeanette.

'Recovery is going to be long and gradual,' he cautioned, as the sisters sat in his cramped office at the Infirmary. 'If your mother continues to regain strength and make steady improvement, we might expect to see her discharged by Christmas — bear in mind though, there can be no guarantees!'

'Not until Christmas?' cried Jeanette in consternation. 'That's still ages away!'

'The weeks will soon go by; and besides, it'll give you time to make ready for your mother's return,' he replied. 'Dorothy's going to be an invalid in need of nursing, girls. Stairs are out of the question, obviously. Is there a ground-floor room you can prepare for her?'

'The back parlour!' chorused the sisters.

'It's a nice, airy room,' added Ellen. 'Ma's always liked it. She does her sewing in there because it gets so much light.'

'We can bring her bed downstairs,' put in Jeanette eagerly. 'And the little bedside cabinet where she keeps her books and knitting.'

'Sounds perfect!' declared Cecil Irwin, rising from his desk. 'We'll organise a wheelchair too, and come next spring when the weather improves, you'll be able to take your mum out and about for a breath of fresh air . . . '

The sisters didn't lose any time in beginning to clear the back parlour of its heavy furniture, and making the comfortable room ready for their mother's homecoming. They visited Dorothy in the Infirmary every day, and although she tired easily and her breathing was still rather laboured, she had plenty to say upon the subject.

' . . . and before the pair of you start,' she murmured, silencing both daughters when they made to protest, 'I mean what I say! I'm not daft. I know I'll have to take things easy when I get out of here, but I've been independent all my life and I'll not be a burden now — '

'Ma! You're not — '

'Hear me out!' She frowned. 'I've been thinking on it. We'll get help for the shop. Maybe young Billy Clough from next door. He's coming up leaving school, and he's a sensible lad who knows shop work backwards.'

Dorothy slowly drew in a difficult breath, fixing her attention upon Ellen before continuing. 'Jeanette and me managed grand before I was poorly, Nellie, and we'll manage again. You've no cause to stay here away from your man and your job.'

'This is where I *want* to be, Ma!' responded Ellen, gripping her mother's bony hand. 'Brian understands, and so does Hathersedge's.'

'Aye, that's as maybe. But you can't expect them to keep your job open forever, and you've worked far too hard to let it go. Don't forget, you've a wedding to get ready for, too!' Dorothy smiled, wearied by the effort of talking so much but pleased she'd set things to rights. 'That's settled then. So, when are you going back to Liverpool and that husband-to-be of yours, Nellie?'

\* \* \*

'Ma's right, you know.' Jeanette was saying on Saturday morning. 'You can't stay here when you have a whole life of your own and a fiancé waiting in Liverpool!'

'Ma's an invalid, Jeanette,' Ellen said tersely. 'She'll be bedridden. Needing care and nursing for months after she comes home.'

'We'll manage,' replied her younger sister calmly. 'You *do* need to go home, Nellie! You can't expect Brian to wait forever.'

'That's not — ' began Ellen, breaking off as a stream of children poured into the shop, setting the brass bell above the door jangling frantically.

Saturday was one of the corner shop's busiest days. Kiddies crowded in clutching pocket money on their way into the Imperial for the children's picture show; regular customers came by to pay their bills; others dropped in to browse the shelves of periodicals and choose their sweets, 'baccy or smokes. There was no further opportunity for the sisters to discuss Ellen's plans until

early afternoon, when the only customers were a woman buying a sensible
present for her grandson's birthday,
and Alex Munro, settling his paper bill
with Ellen while his children were
choosing their Saturday sweets and a
storybook each from the shop's little
shelf of children's tales.

Chilly sunlight was creeping through
the window's small panes as Jeanette
leaned in to replace the box of fountain
pens amongst a display of inks and writing materials. 'Quick, Nellie! It's Barbara
Naylor's wedding going past,' she shouted.
'I wish I could've been at the church to
see her come out! Somebody told me
her dress cost *hundreds!*'

'Fred Naylor's not short of brass,'
sniffed the fountain pen woman, peer-
ing through the window for a good look.
'If a mill-owner can't afford a fancy
frock for his only daughter's wedding,
who can?'

'Oh, it's an absolute *dream*, Nellie!'
Jeanette hurried around to the doorstep, closely followed by little Peggy

Munro and Ellen.

'She does look lovely!' agreed Ellen, a shade wistfully.

The bridal couple were in an flower-bedecked open carriage drawn by two high-stepping white horses, bringing the Saturday shoppers and traffic to a stand-still as the wedding party processed along Market Street towards The Feathers and a sumptuous reception.

'She's like a fairytale princess!' gasped Peggy, wide-eyed behind her big round spectacles. 'I've never seen anyone so beautiful!'

'Hang on, love,' muttered Jeanette, ducking back into the shop to emerge ripping open a small box. 'We must throw some confetti over the bride and groom to wish them luck!'

Peggy cupped her small hands while Jeanette filled them with prettily-tinted tissue-paper horseshoes, hearts and church bells; and together they showered the newlyweds as they clip-clopped by. Radiant with happiness, the bride reached around to one of the posies adorning the carriage and unhooked its ribbons. Beaming down at the serious little girl on the pavement, she gently threw the flowers into her arms.

'Thank you!' cried Peggy, spinning around to look from Jeanette up towards her father. 'Look, Father! Look what the bride gave me!'

'It's very pretty, Peggy.'

'It's also very lucky! Wish I'd caught it! Oh, wasn't it all just too elegant!' laughed Jeanette, turning to her sister and adding, 'Hey, Nellie — that'll be you soon!'

'Hardly!' chuckled Ellen, bending to admire Peggy's posy as they all went back into the shop. 'Our wedding will be more shanks' pony than shining white horses!'

'Are you going to be a bride, Miss Butterworth?' exclaimed Peggy solemnly. 'Are — '

'Peggy!' Alex Munro looked taken aback, his quiet voice unusually sharp. 'Don't be rude. Apologise to Miss Butterworth at once!'

'There's no need, Mr Munro. No harm's done!' replied Ellen airily. His rebuke to the little girl's curiosity irked her, and with another smile she knelt down beside Peggy and nodded happily. 'Yes, Peggy, I'm to be married too! It won't be a grand affair. Just a very quiet wedding with a few friends.'

'Will you have a long white dress and a lacy veil and lots of flowers?' persisted Peggy.

''Fraid not, pet.' She smoothed a wisp of soft brown hair into place beneath Peggy's alice band. 'But a wedding's really about what's in your heart, not frills and flounces.'

Peggy nodded thoughtfully, considering Ellen's bare hands. 'Why haven't you got an engagement ring?'

'Stop bothering Miss Butterworth!' reprimanded the lawyer sternly. 'Go along and choose your book.'

'Rings are very expensive, Peggy,' replied Ellen, ignoring Alex Munro's annoyance. 'My fiancé and I are decorating and furnishing our new home instead. Besides, the only ring I really want is the gold band Brian will give me on our wedding day!'

Peggy nodded, blinking behind her glasses. 'That's very romantic, Miss Butterworth.'

'I think so!' laughed Ellen, looking around to where Robbie was standing by the toy soldiers, looking bored and left out. 'This isn't the sort of thing to interest a boy, is it?'

He shook his head dismally.

Ellen offered her hand and led the small boy towards the glass-fronted counter. 'Have you seen the jelly snakes we've just got in? Or you might like some sherbet dabs or liquorice boot-laces . . . '

When the sisters finally closed up for the night, Barbara Naylor's wedding was still in Jeanette's thoughts. 'We were at school together, you know,' she remarked, sorting the ration coupons they'd taken that day. 'Barbara Naylor and I. When she was about twelve, her mum and dad sent her away to

158

boarding school in Sussex. I believe that's where she met her husband. He's a country squire.'

'Mmm,' answered Ellen, glancing around from tidying the shelves of periodicals. 'I'll finish the coupons, Jen. Why don't you go up and start getting ready?'

'Thanks, Nellie! You're a gem!' whooped Jeanette, giving her sister a hug as she skipped past towards the curtained doorway. 'Why don't you come to the dance with me? It'd do you good to get out and have some fun!'

'And be a wallflower?' chortled Ellen. 'I'm too old for whatever the latest dance craze is now! Besides, I've letters to write, and there's something on the wireless I want to hear.'

While Jeanette was titivating upstairs, Ellen settled at the kitchen table with her notepad. There was plenty of time to think quietly and put pen to paper before *Saturday Night Theatre* began. She wrote two letters: the first to Hilary, bringing her up to date with news of Ma and all that was going on in Whinforth, and the second to Hathersedge's. She then addressed a third envelope to Brian, and with pen poised, began writing.

*My dearest Brian, I'm coming back to Liverpool...*

# 10

'Are you sure you'll be able to manage?' fretted Ellen, clutching her bag and stepping out from the shop.

'Course I am,' replied Jeanette, stamping her feet against the cold and surveying the empty street for any sign of the paper van. 'But are you sure, Nellie? About what you're doing?'

'Positive.'

'It's a huge decision,' persisted Jeanette. 'Turning your whole life upside down just weeks before your wedding. And what does Brian think about it? You've never mentioned that!'

'Brian doesn't know,' responded Ellen in a small voice. 'Oh, Jen! I couldn't tell him in a letter! He's been working such long hours at McBride's, and then going over to fix up the house so it'll be ready for us . . . I need to see him. Talk to him properly.'

Jeanette grimaced. 'Poor Brian!'

'I feel awful about it,' confided Ellen. 'But we came so close to losing Ma! Even after she comes home, it'll be a long while before she's well again. I want to be with her, Jen.'

Jeanette drew a measured breath. 'When Ma finds out you're not going back to Liverpool, she won't be pleased!'

'We're family.' Ellen gave her sister a quick hug before starting toward the bus stop. 'My place is here.'

*   *   *

When Ellen alighted from the train at Lime Street, she was astonished to spot Brian waiting beyond the ticket barrier. She hadn't expected to see him until evening. He was dressed in a snappy business suit, looking every inch the man-about-town, and waving wildly to attract her attention. She broke into a run along the platform and, heedless of the people all around them, allowed herself to be swept into his arms and kissed.

'Oh, queen!' he mumbled thickly, finally releasing her and gazing down into her upturned face. 'You'll never know how bad I've missed you! It's great having you back!'

'I — I didn't expect you to meet me,' she murmured shakily, reeling from the rush of emotions. All her planning and rehearsing how to break the news deserted her. 'I'm glad you're here!'

'Not for long, worse luck!' he grinned, his customary cocksure manner returning as he coiled an arm about her waist and they started from the train station. 'I made an excuse to duck out of the office for half an hour. Now I've seen you, I'll have to leg it back before McBride misses me. What are you doing with yourself for the rest of the day? Seeing Hilary, I suppose. She's a great gal. Worked like mad in the house. You'll hardly know the place when you see it. Curtains, tablecloths and all sorts, ready and waiting for us to move in!'

Ellen swallowed hard, unable to look Brian in the eye. This was horrible.

Listening to him going on about their moving into the house, when she knew full well she'd be returning to Whinforth after the wedding.

She drew breath to just blurt it all out — but how could she? This wasn't the place. He was in a hurry to get back to McBride's. No, she'd keep to her plan and tell him this evening. When they were alone and could talk it over. So Ellen said nothing, merely listened and nodded. Then suddenly she could bear it no longer —

'Brian — there's something I must tell you!' She stopped in her tracks, spinning around to face him. 'I wanted to wait until tonight — '

'Sorry, queen, but it'll have to!' he cut in, bending to touch her lips with a final kiss. 'If I don't get back pronto, McBride will have my guts for garters! See you tonight at our house — it's cracking having you home again!'

'Brian, I'm not back for — '

But another quick kiss and he was gone. Absorbed into a mass of faces thronging the teeming streets and away down toward the waterfront. Dismally, Ellen watched him go. Brian assumed she was back for good. And why wouldn't he? She hadn't written nor told him any different! How could she have let him go on believing she was home? It was cruel and thoughtless!

With heavy heart, she started away from the train station and across town towards Hathersedge's. She'd already written a letter of resignation. All that remained was to make a courtesy visit to Mr Mark at his office, and remove the few personal belongings from her desk, before closing a long and mostly happy chapter of her life.

★　★　★

After Hathersedge's, Ellen's next port of call was Laburnum Avenue. Packing her bags in the large room overlooking the Mersey, and saying a final goodbye to kindly Mrs Cummings, was far more touching than Ellen had anticipated.

She felt near to tears during the bus journey back into town, where she checked her suitcase and holdall into the left luggage office at the train station, ready for her departure to Yorkshire that night.

Pulling herself together, and mindful that Hilary had barely half an hour for lunch, she hurried to the insurance office's building and waited outside for her friend to emerge.

'Nick's put a few tables into a side room at the bakery and made a little café area,' explained Hilary, immediately concerned by her friend's troubled expression. 'It's quiet and the food's good. Shall we eat there?'

'Sounds fine.'

'I've tried asking Nick about your wedding cake,' went on Hilary conversationally, as they made their way to the bakery. 'It's his own secret recipe and he tells me it will be gorgeous, but insists upon it being a surprise on the big day!'

There were two female assistants

behind the bakery's counter; however, Nick himself came forward to show Ellen and Hilary to a table in the café alcove and take their order. When he'd returned to the kitchen, Ellen glanced archly at her companion. 'You and Nick seem very friendly.'

Hilary shrugged. 'I come in here most days. When the bakery isn't busy, we occasionally have a chat.'

'And?'

'And nothing!' Hilary said firmly, as Nick appeared with their lunch and a museum catalogue.

'I've marked the page, Hilary.' He offered her the booklet. 'The exhibition seems well worth a visit, but see what you think.'

'What's all this then?' asked Ellen, when he'd gone. 'What's been happening while I've been away?'

'Nothing at all, Little Miss Match-maker,' replied Hilary patiently. 'Once, when I came into the bakery, Nick was listening to Beethoven on the wireless. We discovered we both enjoy classical music. A few weeks later, there was a concert in Chester; and since we're both on our own, Nick suggested we go together. It was a very enjoyable evening.'

'You're going out together!' cried Ellen. 'Oh, that's marvellous, Hil!'

'We've been on several outings. That's all,' insisted Hilary good-naturedly. 'However, it *is* nice having a companion to share things again!'

'I'm so pleased for you,' Ellen said warmly as they finished lunch and left the bakery. 'You deserve to be happy again!'

'Thank you, Nell. So do you — and you will be. You and Brian together,' she responded softly. 'This separation is difficult, but you'll get through it.

'You have your wedding to look forward to. Brian's arranged everything. The registry office is booked, flowers and champagne ordered, and a nice wedding breakfast in your new home, planned to the last detail. It is a great shame your mother and Jeanette aren't able to come, but perhaps you and Brian could have a blessing later at St. Bede's in Whinforth.'

Ellen was staring directly ahead as they walked. 'Brian met me at the train station today,' she said suddenly. 'He thinks I'm back for good.'

'Then I gather Brian doesn't know you'll be returning to Whinforth after the wedding, either?'

Ellen shook her head miserably. 'I want to be properly married, Hilary! I don't want to leave my husband and my new home to go rushing back to Yorkshire for months on end, but what choice have I?'

'None,' replied Hilary simply. 'You won't be the first couple to marry one day and part the next. It's wretched. Bernard and I had just hours together before he had to rejoin his unit.

'We didn't see each other again for almost three years, but we were *married*, Nell! We each belonged to the other,' she went on softly. 'You and Brian will be apart for a while, but you'll still be husband and wife. That's what matters! And I'll always be glad to go up to Whinforth and lend a hand so you can come down here for a few days.'

'You'd do that?' cried Ellen emotionally. 'You're such a good friend, Hil! I know I shouldn't be complaining, but more than anything in the world I want Brian and I to be together!'

'Your mother will get well and everything will slip back into its proper place, you'll see,' reassured Hilary. 'Meanwhile, have a lovely romantic dinner with Brian this evening, and start looking forward to your wedding — this time next month, you'll be Mrs Brian Kennedy!'

\* \* \*

Mindful that this would be the last occasion she'd see Brian before their wedding day, Ellen took great pleasure shopping for the special meal they'd share that evening. Letting herself in at the tall front door, she marvelled at how very hard Brian and Hilary had worked to make the house homely and comfortable. Afternoon faded into evening as she prepared the meal, and Ellen was just setting a bowl of late flowers in the centre of the dining table when a key turned in the lock.

Brian was home!

Flying along the hall, she got there as the door was swinging open, and expected to be swept into his arms — but froze where she stood.

Brian's face was stony. He turned away from her, shutting the door loudly before rounding on her angrily.

'What the devil's going on, Nellie?' he demanded, shrugging off his overcoat and hat. 'I've just bumped into old Poppleton at the bus stop. He was whinging on about how sorry everybody at Hathersedge's was that you'd left! Course, Soft Lad here hadn't a clue what the smug so-and-so was on about! I felt a right fool, hearing it from the likes of him!'

'I'm so sorry, Brian!' she faltered, just standing and staring. 'I meant to tell you — '

'It's a pity you didn't, then!' he retorted, striding into the front room without even noticing the welcoming fire or attractive table. 'You're going to be my *wife*, Nellie! How come I'm the last to know what you're doing? Why didn't you tell me? You've written enough letters!'

'I tried telling you at the station,' she countered stiffly, taken aback by the virulence of his outburst. 'If you'd like to wash your hands and sit down, I'll dish up before our supper spoils.'

The fire and lamplight were casting flickering shadows across the beautifully-proportioned room when Ellen served the meal. Apparently oblivious to the good food and romantic atmosphere, Brian sat grimly at one end of the table and they ate in silence. It wasn't until Ellen brought in the marmalade pudding and was setting down the dishes that Brian reached across the table and caught her fingers.

'This is great, Nellie. The food and everything,' he mumbled, gazing shamefaced up into her cool eyes. 'I'm sorry I flew off the handle about old Popinjay. You know me, I open my big mouth before I use my brains! My pride was hurt. That him and the rest of that smarmy lot at Hathersedge's knew what you were doing before I did. Actually, I'm glad you've packed it in. I know you liked your little job, but I never was happy with the notion of you working after we're wed.'

He stood up, taking her slowly into his arms. 'Don't stay mad at me, queen! I was bang out of order, and I admit it. Truth is, I've been edgy ever since you went away.' He bent to kiss her lips. 'You're back now. That's the main thing.'

'Brian,' murmured Ellen when finally they parted. Taking a steadying breath, she stepped slightly away from him. 'You don't understand. I'm not back. Not for good, anyhow. That's why I had to leave Hathersedge's. I'm catching the late train to Whinforth tonight.'

'You're what?' he exploded in disbelief, raking a hand through his shock of red hair. 'But you've only just got here! How long will you be away this time?'

'I don't know,' she answered, turning away to take her seat at the table. 'Not for certain.'

'But your mam's getting better! Why have you got to go back?'

'I can't leave Jeanette on her own.'

He exhaled heavily and sat back in the chair, staring at her. 'I suppose a few more weeks won't make much difference — won't have to, will it? — and you'll surely have the shop sorted out by then.'

Ellen swallowed hard. Her mouth was dry. 'It isn't only the shop. Ma will be an invalid when she first gets out of hospital. She'll need us to look after her.'

'Exactly what are you saying, Nellie?' he challenged, his dark eyes boring into her. 'That even after we're wed, you plan on going back to Yorkshire?'

'I've no choice, Brian!' she returned passionately. 'My family needs me!'

'What about me, Nellie? Your husband! Don't I count?' he retaliated curtly. 'When your mam was taken bad, it was obvious you wanted to be on hand, but now . . . What if we were already married? Would your family still expect you to drop everything and go running home?'

'My mother and Jeanette both want me to return to Liverpool,' replied Ellen coldly, rising from the table and resting her fingertips on the edge of the smooth linen cloth. 'Staying in Whinforth is my choice. I'm needed at home, Brian,' she added quietly. 'You must see that.'

'Hobson's choice, isn't it?' he retorted bitterly, scraping back his chair. 'What's the point in us getting wed at all?'

Ellen was horrified. Struggling to find words to make him understand.

'I love you and I want to be your wife, Brian! Being apart is awful, but it's only a temporary setback. When you were at sea, we were separated for months and months on end — and by much greater distance than from here to Whinforth!'

'I couldn't walk out of the Navy just because it suited me,' he snapped curtly. 'It was my job, for pity's sake!'

'Yes, it was. And for the time being, helping Jeanette and caring for Ma is mine.' she said calmly, her composure regained. 'Try to see it from my viewpoint, Brian. It's only reasonable — '

'I'm sick to the back teeth of being reasonable!' he cut in harshly. 'This just isn't on, Nellie. It's not on!'

'But you know how much I love you — '

'Do I? Prove it, Nellie!' he slammed the palm of his hand flat upon the table, setting the crockery rattling. 'Because from where I'm standing, it doesn't look like it!

'I've been here night after night getting our home ready for us. Now you tell me you won't be coming to live in it with me.' he strode from the room, snatching his coat from the hook and wrenching open the front door. 'You've got to choose, Nellie. Either you put us and our marriage first, or there won't be any wedding!'

★ ★ ★

The silence of the house weighed heavily.

Ellen was shocked and angered by Brian's ultimatum as she washed and tidied away the supper dishes. He was wrong and unfair demanding such a thing! How could she do anything but return to Yorkshire? She wandered about the house for what she realised was probably the last time. Brian wasn't the kind of man to back down. Somehow, Ellen knew she'd never set foot here again. It was over. All over.

Giving way to the heartache and despair, she wrapped her arms across her chest and stopped trying to stem the bitter tears that had threatened since the front door slammed. Methodically dousing the fires, she went around turning out the gas lamps, leaving just the one in the hall to light her departure. Buttoning her coat against the chill autumnal night, Ellen finally snuffed that light too, plunging the house into utter blackness.

Stepping out onto the steps, she paused, looking back at the shining windows and in her mind's eye seeing the comfortable rooms within. The home where she would have become Brian's wife and had his children. Squeezing the key tight within her hand for one last time, Ellen noiselessly closed the door and slipped the key through the letter-box before turning away towards town and the train station.

She didn't hurry. There was plenty of time. Nevertheless, she reached Lime Street all too soon, and made straight for the left luggage office to retrieve her bags.

'Nellie!'

Swinging around, she watched in disbelief as Brian sprinted towards her.

'Wasn't sure what time your train

went — ' he began sheepishly, standing squarely before her. 'I've been waiting ages.'

Ellen considered him warily, her emotions spent.

'I couldn't let you go like this,' he began when she didn't speak. 'Didn't want us to break up that way.' He nodded toward the tea room. 'How about a cuppa? It's late, but I reckon they'll still have some of that jollop that passes for tea.'

Wearily, Ellen shook her head. 'I don't think so, Brian. I just want to go home.'

'At least sit down a minute! There's time before your train, I've checked the board,' he urged, taking her arm and leading her to the bench beneath the station clock. 'I apologise, Nellie. I lose my rag and say stuff I shouldn't. Always have. That's my trouble.'

'Things are as they are, Brian. My family needs me and I don't intend on letting them down. I'm sorry if you don't understand that.'

'Look, queen. I've never had any family worth mentioning, but it's different with you. I realise that — now I've stopped seeing red,' he admitted. 'The idea of us being married and you hundreds of miles away for God knows how long kicked the guts out of me.'

'It is a shock,' conceded Ellen with a heavy sigh. 'I'd wanted to explain things properly.'

Brian took her hands and held them tight. 'I've had time to cool my heels and think. Suppose we postpone the wedding? Put it off until your mam is well enough to come down here with your sister and see us get hitched?'

'Postpone . . . ' echoed Ellen in a small voice, trying to marshal her thoughts. 'Yes. Yes, I expect that would be best.'

'I'll sort everything this end, and we'll rearrange it all when your mam's up and about, eh?' he continued positively. 'Start afresh, sort of.'

Distractedly, she glanced above them to the clock and stood up. 'I have to collect my luggage.'

'I'll get it . . .'

With her belongings safely stowed on the rack in the empty compartment, she and Brian stood alone, staring at each other wordlessly.

The noise of the great engine gathering steam was deafening and the shouts of porters and guards even louder in the empty, echoing station.

Hesitantly, Brian touched her cheek with his fingertips. 'I'm going to miss you!'

Drawing her into his arms, he held her against him. Determined not to cry, Ellen squeezed her eyes tight shut and rested her cheek against the smooth weave of his overcoat, clinging to him as if this were indeed their last goodbye. The whistle blew. Brian reluctantly stepped from her. Turning on his heel, he strode from the compartment and along the corridor, leaping down onto the deserted platform.

Glancing back over his shoulder, he raised a hand in reluctant farewell.

'Come back to me soon, Nellie!'

# 11

Autumn ebbed towards winter; by mid-November, the back parlour was freshly-papered and -painted in readiness for Dorothy's homecoming, and the first boxes of festive stock were arriving at the Butterworths' corner shop. Ellen had spoken little about her postponed wedding plans, and although tact wasn't her strong point, Jeanette had followed suit — until the morning she could remain silent no longer!

'I do think you're brave, Nellie!' she exploded, turning around with a bundle of brightly-coloured crêpe paper in her arms and looking across to where Ellen was arranging a display of Christmas cards. 'This must be a pig of a day for you!'

'I admit, I do keep thinking — what if . . . ?' replied Ellen ruefully. 'But Brian was absolutely right about putting it off.

Without you and Ma there to see me married, it wouldn't have felt like a proper wedding day anyhow.'

'Even so,' grimaced Jeanette, adding vaguely, 'Brian doesn't write much, does he?'

Ellen laughed at that. 'My fiancé has many talents, but being a man of letters definitely isn't among them!'

'I can't wait to meet him!' Jeanette dived into a box of cotton-wool snowmen with jaunty felt hats and bright button eyes. 'He *will* be coming for Christmas, won't he?'

Ellen frowned slightly. 'Do you know, Brian and I have never once spent Christmas together? He's always been at sea before, and now he's ashore I'm not certain he'll get time off!'

'On Christmas Day?' snorted Jeanette. 'Jack McBride must be a proper Scrooge!'

'He's a businessman. A very successful one,' commented Ellen. 'If Mr McBride wants Brian in the office, he'll have to be there.'

'That's rotten! Poor Brian!' cried

Jeanette impulsively. 'Still, it is a really good job, isn't it?'

'Considering Brian hasn't been at the shipping office for very long, Mr McBride does delegate to him a great deal,' remarked Ellen proudly.

'This McBride is getting on a bit, isn't he? I bet when he retires, he puts Brian in charge of the whole shebang!'

'From the little I've seen of Jack McBride, he doesn't seem the retiring type!' laughed Ellen. 'Besides, Brian's determined to start his own business as soon as he can.'

'Oh, I remember you saying that! He's right, of course. You can't beat a proper family business. I wouldn't want to go and work for somebody else!'

'Brian's greatly impressed with his old shipmate's success. Nick — Nick the baker, Hilary's friend — left the Navy and opened his own bakery. He's expanded into a little café now, too. He's doing very well and Brian's determined to do the same. Being his own boss and having something of his

own is terribly important to him — '
She broke off as the door opened and
Doctor Irwin entered. The physician
never came into the shop this late in the
day!

'Doctor! What's happened?'

'Why have you come?' demanded
Jeanette. 'What's wrong?'

'Can't a poor old man call in for two
ounces of extra-strong peppermints
without being greeted like the spectre
of doom?' he queried, smiling broadly
and immediately allaying their fears.
'How's that back parlour of yours
coming along?'

'All done!' grinned Jeanette, catching
his cheery mood. 'Ready and waiting.'

'That's very fortuitous, because I've
seen your mother this morning and told
her she can come home next week.'

'That's wonderful news!' exclaimed
Ellen. 'We'd been keeping our fingers
crossed Ma would be here in time for
Christmas!'

'Dorothy continues to make steady
progress and, to be honest, we need the

bed,' he replied ruefully. 'Winter's setting in fast and admissions are rising, especially amongst the old and needy. Besides, as you well know, your mum's eager to be out of that hospital and back home with you both.'

'You're sure Ma's strong enough to come out?' persisted Ellen cautiously.

'I'd never discharge her otherwise, Nellie,' replied the doctor mildly. 'What she needs most now is rest and building up, and she'll get that here with the pair of you clucking around like mother hens. I'll look in every day at first, so you need have no worries.

'Now, is there any possibility of a weary old sawbones getting his bag of extra-strong peppermints . . . ?'

Between customers, the sisters cracked on with unpacking new stock and decorating the bright little shop. Ellen was up the step-ladder, on tiptoe, pinning up plump twists of festive paper garlands.

'Are these straight, Jen?' she asked, leaning back as far as she dared to survey the red, gold and green garlands with which she was festooning the ceiling's four corners. 'They look a bit wonky to me?'

Stepping backwards to gain a better perspective, Jeanette narrowed her eyes and considered. 'Spot on, Nellie! Straight as an arrow — oh, sorry, Alex! Didn't mean to back into you!'

'My fault entirely, Jeanette!' he exclaimed apologetically, glancing up from the exercise book he was holding in his hand. 'I wasn't looking where I was going when I came in.'

'What do you think?' she asked, her attention returning to the Christmas decorations. 'There are still shortages of course, but so much more festive stuff is available this year. It's almost back to normal like before the war. Nellie thought the garlands and holly and angels and those strings of dancing silver stars might be a bit too much, but I say you can't have too much of a good thing at Christmastime!'

'Indeed.' He nodded, gazing up to

where Ellen was still balanced atop the step-ladder. 'Although, if I may say so, I think perhaps just a fraction higher to the left?'

'Exactly what I thought!' replied Ellen, making the adjustment and climbing down the ladder. 'What can I get you, Mr Munro?'

'I've a considerable list. Oh, but first of all, may I have *The Rainbow* and Peggy's *Girls' Crystal*, an ounce of my usual mixed flake, a packet of pipe-cleaners and a box of matches, please?'

Ellen gathered together the items while Alex Munro read through a neatly-written list in the exercise book, setting it onto the counter so she might see. 'We need a plentiful supply of crêpe paper, glue, paste brushes, frieze paper, card, water paints — '

'You're making Christmas decorations!' laughed Ellen, glancing at the list. 'My word, your children are going to enjoy this!'

'Actually, it's not for us. At home, I mean,' he replied, his brow creasing.

'No, it's for the school.'

'Ah-ha! Miss Thwaite's made you one of Santa's little elves, hasn't she?' exclaimed Jeanette with a wide grin. 'Same here! I've been pressed into service to help out at the schoolchildren's Christmas party, and she's roped in Stephen and some of the other boys to find a suitable tree and Yule log. You'll be next, Nellie!'

'I'll be glad to lend a hand!' she laughed, returning her attention to Alex Munro. 'How much will you need?'

'Lots,' he replied wryly. 'You see, as a gesture of gratitude for the school allowing us use of their hall and facilities, the Players always provide craft materials so the pupils can deck their classrooms and make Christmas gifts to take home. We also decorate the assembly hall and the tree . . . I'm afraid I don't have much imagination for this sort of thing.'

He was gazing hopefully across the counter at her, and Ellen nodded slowly. 'Mmm, so as well as what's on the list, you could do with garlands, paper lanterns, a few baubles maybe. Some candles and lights, perhaps?'

'Excellent!' he exclaimed gratefully. 'Thank you so much for your help, Miss Butterworth.'

'You're welcome! We'll send off the order today, and should have it all in for you next week.'

'Splendid, splendid!' He touched his hat politely, gathering up his purchases. 'Good afternoon, ladies.'

There was a steady trickle of customers for a while, so the sisters had no opportunity for discussing Ma's homecoming, decorating the shop, or unpacking the heavy boxes of wooden toys made by wounded veterans in the servicemen's home over at Gylbeck.

It was almost closing time, and Ellen was counting the takings, when Jeanette made a start on opening the boxes.

'These toys from the servicemen are terrific! Have you ever seen such workmanship?' she exclaimed, carefully removing layers of protective straw and revealing handmade horses and carts, trains and jointed dolls. Suddenly Jeanette sat back on her heels, holding up an exquisitely-carved Nativity stable so Ellen might see.

'Isn't this beautiful, Nellie — and won't it be lovely to have Ma home again?' she whispered, her blue eyes sparkling. 'We're going to have the best Christmas ever, aren't we?'

★ ★ ★

Dorothy was looking brighter by the day, and taking increasing interest in everything that went on in the shop. When the back parlour door was left ajar, she could hear snatches of conversation, and was keen to catch up with the steady stream of news and town gossip that flowed over the counter.

Nevertheless, illness had left her weak, and despite being confined to bed, Dorothy tired easily and took frequent naps. After she'd eaten a light midday meal, Ellen cleared away the dishes and settled down at her mother's bedside to read aloud another couple of chapters from the latest whodunnit borrowed from the library. Presently, Dorothy's eyelids grew heavy, and when she'd drifted into sleep, Ellen closed the novel and crept out, leaving the door open so her mother could call if she wakened and needed anything.

'This icy weather is certainly keeping a lot of folk indoors.' remarked Jeanette, glancing up from the pages of *Red Letter* when Ellen came through into the shop. 'We've been quiet all day. I'll miss Hilary being with us for Christmas, won't you? Still, it's smashing she's spending it with her chap and his family.'

'Yes. Yes, it is,' agreed Ellen, shoving aside the bulky cardboard boxes that had been delivered earlier. 'She's already been up to Haithe on several occasions, and met Nick's parents and his married sister and niece and nephews. Hilary says Nick's family are really nice and friendly. She sounded very pleased and excited to be invited to stay with them for Christmas.'

'Must be serious!' mused Jeanette mischievously. 'Do you think they'll tie the knot?'

'I don't know,' answered Ellen thoughtfully. 'Their romance seems to have blossomed since I've been away. It'd be wonderful if Nick is the one, though. Hilary has been alone and lonely far too long. She's deserves to be happy again, and I know she'd dearly love to have a family of her own.'

'A double wedding next year then?' suggested Jeanette artfully. 'You and Brian, and Hilary and Nick?'

'We'd certainly have the best wedding cakes — ouch!' she yelped, stubbing her toes against the stack of cumbersome boxes. 'These are in the way! I'll take them up to the school when we close. Miss Thwaite's given me a key.'

'Why not go now? We're not exactly run off our feet here, and Ma'll be asleep for ages yet,' remarked Jeanette, stooping to sort the boxes into two piles. 'Just take the children's craft materials this afternoon, and we'll take the rest between us when we go to rehearsals tomorrow night. I'm really looking forward to all the Players decorating the Christmas tree and the hall, aren't you? Miss Thwaite is bringing hot mulled punch and mince pies!'

The December afternoon was already closing in to dusk when Ellen unloaded the craft boxes from her bicycle and, with the help of a chirpy female teacher about her own age, stowed them into the school stockroom.

'This is a grand selection of materials!' enthused the young woman, taking a peek. 'The children'll have a fine time making all their Christmassy things — you and the rest of the Players have done us proud, Miss Butterworth!'

Pleased, Ellen was still smiling as she pushed her bicycle across the deserted schoolyard towards the tall gates. Several women bundled against the bitter weather were gathering outside, and Ellen waved cheerfully in response to Ada Heggie's call just as a muffled bell clanged the end of another schoolday.

'How's your ma?'

'Doing well, Ada,' beamed Ellen, moving her bicycle aside as the first rush of youngsters erupted through the gates. 'But you know Ma, she can't abide being idle! Now she's feeling a bit better, she wants to be doing things. Jeanette caught her sitting up in bed sorting out her knitting basket the other day!'

'Ah, that's a good sign!' declared the little woman, balancing her laden shopping baskets on the low wall. 'Tell your mum I've a grand pattern for a fancy cardy she might like to knit. It's got stitches like seashells down the edges. I've just finished making one for my niece over in York.

'I'd like nowt better than to visit your ma. When she's up to visitors, that is.'

'She'd be delighted to see you any

time, Ada,' responded Ellen at once. 'You're always welcome, you know that.'

'And how are you getting on?' asked the elderly woman bluntly. 'Must be hard, being separated from your man. He's coming up for Christmas, I take it?'

Ellen hesitated, glancing past Ada to the happy children spilling from the school doors. 'I'm not certain yet. Brian may have to work at Christmastime.'

'I see,' was all Ada said. 'Well, there'll be plenty going on in Whinforth to keep your spirits up. You'll be joining in with the candlelight carol-singing, I suppose?'

'Well, I — '

'Oh, you must, lass! You and Jeanette both. Jeanette always goes along. I can't sing a note, so I stay away, but it's a grand night,' she went on. 'I'll keep Dorothy company while you and Jeanette go off carolling. Ah, here they come — the little ragamuffins!'

'They seem very nice children,' smiled Ellen, spotting the brother and sister coming down the stone steps.

'Oh, they're grand bairns!' declared Ada fiercely. 'I just wish they had a bit more fun, y'know? Mr Munro does his best, bless him, but he doesn't have much idea when it comes to kiddies playing and having fun. Oh, I know some folk think Mr Munro's a bit dour, but he's not really. He's a dear man. He's just . . . quiet. Shy, sort of.'

Ada's face lit up as Peggy and Robbie came hurtling across the yard towards her.

'I wrote on the board!' shouted Robbie, wrapping his arms about the elderly woman and gazing up into her rosy round face. 'I wrote my name on the board in big letters!'

'You never did! Fancy that, eh?' replied Ada, tousling his dark hair and looking to Peggy, standing quietly beside Ellen's bicycle. 'What about you, pet? Have you had a nice day at school?'

'We're going to make paper chains for our classroom tomorrow. And Christmas presents to take home, too,' she replied, turning to Ellen. 'Miss Patterson showed us the coloured papers and paints and sparkly stuff Father ordered from your shop, Miss Butterworth.'

'I've just this minute delivered them!' said Ellen, smiling down at the solemn little girl. 'What sort of presents are you going to make?'

'I'll make cards for Father and Mrs Heggie and Robbie and Miss Patterson,' answered Peggy thoughtfully. 'Then I'll make a calendar for Father to put on his desk in his office. It's a surprise.' she added, looking Ellen straight in the eye.

'Won't breathe a word! I'm very good at keeping secrets — ' She broke off, seeing Ada lifting the heavy shopping baskets onto her arms. 'I'll put those on my bike and walk back with you!'

'Are you sure you don't mind?' queried the little woman. 'I don't want to keep you from getting back to your ma.'

Ellen shook her head, already loading the baskets. 'Ma's having her afternoon nap, and the shop's very quiet today.'

'Plenty folk don't like being out when it's icy,' replied Ada, taking Peggy and Robbie's hands as they started away towards the river. 'They're frightened of slipping. I am myself. Had a bad fall some thirty years back and broke my foot. It's never been right since.' She indicated her right foot with its thick woollen stocking and sturdy shoe. 'See how it's a bit wonky? And the ankle's thicker than t'other? Still, I get about alright on it so I can't complain.

'By, that's a keen wind coming down from the hills!' She shivered as the drovers' bridge spanning the swift, cold waters of the Whin came into sight. 'When we get to Lane End House, will you have time to come in for a warm and a cuppa . . . ?'

★   ★   ★

'You're going, Nellie,' said Dorothy firmly, smoothing down the folds in her counterpane. 'And there's an end to it!'
'Ma, I won't be missing anything if I

don't go!' protested Ellen in exasperation. It was the week before Christmas and the play's opening night. 'I've seen it all the way through at dress rehearsal. I'd much rather stay here with you.'

'I'd much rather you didn't!' returned her mother sharply. 'You've worked hard behind the scenes, Nellie. Sewing costumes and painting scenery, dressing the tree and decorating the hall, not to mention putting up posters and selling tickets. You should be there tonight to enjoy the fruits of your labours.'

'I'd worry about your being alone,' murmured Ellen at last. 'And Ada can't come down because she's looking after Peggy and Robbie.'

'Eee, I don't need a babysitter!' Dorothy frowned. 'Anyhow, there's no cause for me to be on my own if that's all that's stopping you. Beattie from next door has her sister Rita up from Stafford for Christmas. The three of us were best friends at school, but we haven't seen each other for years, and we're just waiting for a chance to get together and catch up. Give Beattie a knock and ask her and Rita to drop round this evening. Then you can dig out your glad rags and get yourself ready — if you can prise Jeanette out of the bathroom!'

'It *is* her big night, and she's only been in there three hours!' grinned Ellen, brushing her mother's forehead with a quick kiss. 'Thanks, Ma. I'll go next door and then storm the bathroom!'

The school's austere assembly hall was transformed by swags of glossy holly and ivy, silver bells and gaily-coloured garlands, and the fragrant blue-green spruce — decked with shimmering glass baubles and brightly sparkling fairy-lights, crowned by a glittering crystal angel. There wasn't an empty seat in the house, and Ellen was sitting on a short front row alongside Eunice Thwaite, Alex Munro and other members of the Players who weren't in the cast.

She had a fine view, and felt as though she held her breath from the moment the curtain went up until it finally came down after no fewer than five encores. Jeanette and the others had been magnificent!

'Wasn't it wonderful!' exclaimed Ellen, turning to Alex as the lights went on and he started packing away the photographic equipment. 'The sets and costumes looked so beautiful, too. You must've got some smashing pictures!'

'I hope so!' he smiled, carefully fitting the camera into its padded case. 'I always take plenty and pass them all onto the editor at the *Clarion* so he can select which ones to put in the paper. You're absolutely right about it being a beautiful production, though. And that's in no short measure to your own hard work. The stage was exquisitely dressed.'

'Thank you!' smiled Ellen, taken aback by the compliment. 'I wish Ma had been here with us! She'd love to see Jeanette up there on stage and would've been so very proud of her tonight!'

'After the Christmas break, there'll be another half-dozen performances in the New Year. Perhaps by then . . . '

Alex paused thoughtfully, going on. 'Meanwhile, I can easily have an extra set of prints developed for Mrs Butterworth. At least she'll have a taste of the performance, and quite a number of the pictures include Jeanette.'

'That's very generous, Mr Munro!' exclaimed Ellen, beaming. 'Thank you so much!'

'My pleasure,' he murmured, smiling hesitantly down at her. 'I could have the best of them enlarged and framed, as a sort of souvenir of Jeanette's first play — if you think your mother might like that?'

'Like it? She'd be thrilled!' exclaimed Ellen in delight. 'It's a lovely thought, Mr Munro, and so very kind of you.'

'I'll have them developed straight away,' he said, helping her on with her warm coat before putting on his own overcoat and hat. 'As soon as they're ready, I'll bring them by the shop — '

'Well done, one and all!' boomed Eunice Thwaite, emerging from back-stage and striding towards her seat. 'A resounding success, what? Couldn't have gone any better! Jeanette's just getting out of her costume, Ellen. You're both coming across to the coffee-house for a spot of celebrating, aren't you? You too, Alex?'

'I'm afraid not. The children made me promise to come straight home after the play and tell them all about it,' he replied seriously, tipping his hat to the two ladies. 'They were determined to stay awake, and although I'm certain they'll be fast asleep by now, a promise is a promise, so I'd better go. 'Night, Eunice. Goodnight, Miss Butterworth. Enjoy the celebrations.'

'We will indeed!' barked Miss Thwaite, adding with a guffaw, 'I daresay we'll raise a cup or two of eggnog, eh Ellen?'

Although it was very late when the sisters returned to the shop, from the laughter, conversation and light spilling from the back parlour, it was evident Dorothy's childhood reunion was still in full swing.

'I'll put the kettle on for fresh tea, let

Ma know we're back,' grinned Ellen. 'And then leave them to it!'

'From the way they're carrying on,' yawned Jeanette, shrugging off her coat and boots and making for the stairs, 'they'll still be going strong when the morning papers come — oh, I forgot to tell you. The last post came just as we were going out. There's one for you. From Brian, I think. I put it behind the clock on the dresser. Bags me first for the bathroom!'

Ellen lost no time in retrieving the letter. It was from Brian! She caught her breath. It had been such a long while since she'd last heard from him. Smoothing her fingers across the small square envelope, Ellen was torn between the impulse to rip it open and see what he had to say, and saving the letter until later when she could sit quietly in her room and read it slowly, savouring every single line. Deliberately slipping the envelope into the pocket of her skirt, Ellen set to putting cups and saucers onto trays and making tea.

Leaving a cup on Jeanette's bedside table, she took her own into her room and curled up with her letter on the seat in the window. Opening it, she unfolded the single sheet of lined notepaper with a tingle of anticipation. Could it be that Brian was coming to Whinforth for Christmas Day . . . ?

*Dear Nellie,*

*I can't stop thinking we'd be wed by now. But things are as they are, and we'll just have to make the best of it. Jack McBride's just had one of his ships refitted and he wants somebody aboard on her first voyage out to check everything's spot-on. I wanted the berth and he give it me. It's good money, Nellie. It'll get us off to a good start. And it'll be good to feel a deck under my feet one last time.*

*Working for McBride has taught me a lot about running a business. Me and Nick have done a lot of talking too. The more I see of them, the more I want to be my own boss.*

*I've given up the house. There was no point keeping it on and paying rent for something we don't need. To be honest, I'll be glad to get away from Liverpool. I had enough of the place when I was a lad. I'd never have come back when I got out of the Navy, only you were here. Without you, there's nothing to keep me here, so I may as well take the chance and go away.*

*When I get back, I'll be looking to start afresh. I'm thinking of taking a look around your neck of the woods. I've never been to Yorkshire. Nick reckons there might be better prospects there than here for a bloke starting up on his own. I can turn my hand to pretty much anything and I'm a quick learner, if nothing else. I've had to be.*

*We sail the Monday before Christmas for Lisbon...*

In consternation, Ellen searched the letter for a date but Brian hadn't written one. The envelope was post-marked more than a week ago, its delivery most probably delayed in the festive post.

Brian had already sailed for Portugal. He was gone.

Ellen's fingers were trembling, her stomach in knots as she scanned the final lines.

*I wish I could see you once more before I sail, Nellie, but it's all a rush here,* he concluded. *Hopefully next Christmas we'll be together for keeps. Here's to whatever the New Year brings...*

# 12

'I'm always glad to see the tail-end of January,' remarked Ada Heggie, taking off her coat and sitting beside Dorothy's bed in the back parlour. 'At least we haven't had as much snow as last year. I'd never seen snow like it!'

'Nobody had,' replied Dorothy, glancing up from her knitting. 'There's fresh tea in the pot there, Nellie's just made it. Parkin, too.'

'They're grand little cooks, both your girls,' said Ada, dipping into her capacious handbag and taking out a small paper packet. 'Here's the buttons you wanted. I got the pearly sort.'

'They're a perfect match for the wool.' Dorothy put a button against the lilac cardigan sleeve on her needles. 'I'm right pleased with them!'

'Have you tried it?' asked Ada, topping up Dorothy's cup before pouring one for herself.

'Tried what?'

'Yon chair.' She sipped her tea and nodded at the wheelchair in the corner. 'It's come, I see.'

'Pah! The ugly contraption's been sat there days. It's neither use nor ornament!' returned Dorothy in disgust. 'There's Doctor Irwin saying I'm to stay in bed and not try getting up yet, and the girls telling me I've to be patient and not do too much too soon, else it'll set me back! I'm used to keeping busy, Ada. All this resting will see me off!'

'That's a shame,' commented her friend, savouring the parkin. 'I daresay all you'd need is somebody to put the chair alongside your bed. And somebody to help you budge from one to t'other.'

The two women's eyes met.

'I daresay that'd do it,' agreed Dorothy.

* * *

'Good grief, Ma!' yelped Jeanette, whirling around as Dorothy emerged through the curtained doorway into the shop. She was clad in a neat jumper over her nightgown, and had a thick plaid wrapped across her knees and feet. 'What do you think you're doing?'

'What do you *both* think you're doing?' added Ellen with a disapproving glance to Ada Heggie. 'This could set — '

' — me back months, aye, so I've been told. Dozens of times,' interrupted Dorothy briskly. 'I'm the one as knows how I feel, and Ada's the only one who's paid heed. We're going back inside to hear our programme, but from now on it'll do no harm for me to come into the shop sometimes, and find out what's going on in the world!'

'About turn, then!' announced Ada, shoving the unwieldy chair forwards and then changing her mind. 'Nay, back'ards might be best. Keep your elbows in, Dot!'

'Let me give you a push!' cried Ellen,

snatching a block of *Five Boys* from the counter as she hurried by. 'And here's some chocolate to keep your strength up while you're listening to your serial!'

In no time, the two women were ensconced in the back parlour once more, making inroads into the chocolate and waiting for the wireless to warm up.

'Thanks, Ada,' said Dorothy, sorting out her pillows. 'You did grand manoeuvring that chair.'

'Nothing to it, once you get the hang of it,' she replied, fiddling with the wireless and tuning out the crackles. 'There, that's better! Another piece of chocolate, Dot?'

★　★　★

'Nellie, the queerest thing's just happened — golly, something smells good!' Jeanette burst into the kitchen, sweeping off her hat and scarf and setting down a bundle of gramophone records and sheet music onto the dresser.

'You'll never guess who I saw when I was coming out from the music shop!'

'Frank Sinatra going in?' hazarded Ellen, tipping chopped leeks into the bubbling stew pan. 'Or Henry Hall, perhaps?'

'Much queerer than that!' she retorted loftily, her cheeks rosy with cold and excitement. 'I've just seen your Brian's doppelgänger — unless Brian Kennedy really *is* here in Whinforth, that is!'

'I only wish he were!' grimaced Ellen, turning to the table and measuring flour for dumplings. 'Unfortunately, Brian won't get here for another four days.'

'I swear this man was the absolute image of the picture you have on your bedside table. And you have to admit, there aren't too many men around as good-looking as your Brian!' went on Jeanette, dipping into the bowl where dried apple was soaking, and nibbling one of the softening rings. 'He was very smartly-dressed, with wavy red hair and a real jaunty spring in his step like you said Brian has.

'We almost bumped into each other as I came out of the music shop. Then he crossed over and went into the bank. What do you think about that!'

'They do say everyone's got a double,' commented Dorothy, catching the gist of the conversation as she slowly wheeled through the kitchen doorway. 'Although I've never understood how that can be. Shall I put the apples in the pie-dish — if Jeanette hasn't eaten them all?'

'Oops, sorry!' exclaimed Jeanette sheepishly, twirling away to retrieve her purchases from the dresser. 'I got most of the music Miss Thwaite asked for, and some smashing records too!'

'Put them on, Jen,' said Dorothy, steering the clumsy chair with difficulty alongside the table. 'We'll have some music while we work!'

'I'll play my favourite first, it's *As Time Goes By* from *Casablanca*.' She disappeared into the back parlour where the gramophone stood, and a few minutes later came swaying into the kitchen. 'We've got to choose three songs from Hollywood movies so Miss Thwaite can make a list. Then we'll all decide which ones go into the show. Have you chosen yours yet, Nellie?'

'It wouldn't be fitting,' she replied, rolling pastry. 'After all, I'm not a proper member of the Players.'

'But you help out such a lot, nobody would mind!' declared Jeanette. 'Besides, I think it's high time you *did* join!'

'She's right,' put in Dorothy, layering the apple rings. 'You enjoy going to the Players. And there's no need to fret about leaving me on my own anymore. I get about handy in my chair, and can always knock on the wall for Beattie if I need anything. You really should join up, Nellie. Just while you're here in Whinforth.'

Ellen considered. Ma was right. She *had* enjoyed helping out and being a small part of all the fun and bustle. 'Perhaps I will!'

'Good egg!' declared Jeanette, going on excitedly. 'We're auditioning at the next meeting. If I get chosen to do a solo, will you help me make over a frock? It'll have to be super-snazzy for our 'Songs from Hollywood' musical evening!'

On Thursday morning, Jeanette was chirpy as a lark and still bubbling after the previous night's auditions.

'Imagine, Nellie — I'm actually going to sing a solo! And a duet, too.' She pulled a face. 'But with Alex Munro, of all people!'

'Mr Munro's in the choir at St. Bede's,' remarked Ellen distractedly, her thoughts caught up with meeting Brian at the bus stop later that morning. 'And I heard him playing the organ on several occasions when Mr Oldroyd had bronchitis. He must be musical.'

'Alex's a tenor, and to be fair, he does have a decent voice,' conceded Jeanette, putting on the lights and opening up the shop. 'But fancy having to sing Alice Faye's glorious love song from *Hello, Frisco, Hello* with an old stuffed shirt like him! I ask you!'

Ellen was only half-listening by now. There was an unfamiliar fluttering of nerves in her tummy, and an apprehension about seeing Brian she'd never before experienced. But this separation had been different, hadn't it . . . She stirred from her uneasy thoughts, realising Jeanette was speaking to her.

'Hmm? Sorry, Jen! What did you say?'

'I suppose you're entitled to be a bit doolally today!' teased Jeanette with a wide grin. 'If I was being reunited with that dishy fiancé of yours in a couple of hours, I'd be at sixes and sevens too! I was only talking about Alex Munro, anyhow. I mean, just because he sings in church doesn't mean he's got what it takes to sing a romantic duet, does it?'

'A good voice is a good voice,' commented Ellen vaguely, starting to mark up the papers. 'What did he sing for his audition?'

Jeanette grimaced. 'Some awful operatic piece about a tiny frozen hand! It was alright, I suppose. In its way. But it certainly wasn't romantic, Nellie — and I've got to sing *You'll Never Know Just How Much I Love You* with him at the musical evening!'

★ ★ ★

Ellen got to the bus stop in plenty of time, and sat on the bench facing the Great War memorial, thankful for a few quiet minutes to settle her turbulent emotions. Then she spied the bus trundling down between the Dow Hills and over the bridge spanning the swift-flowing Whin. When it swung around to a halt, Ellen spotted Brian at once, and all her uneasiness melted into joy as he blew her a kiss through the grimy window.

'You're a sight for sore eyes, queen!' He was down the step and sweeping her up into his arms right there in the middle of the town. 'I've missed you something terrible!'

'I'm so glad you've come!' she breathed, searching his strong face. 'It seems a lifetime since we've been together!'

'Don't I know it!' he mumbled thickly, kissing her again. 'Ay, can we get had up for doing this sort of thing at the bus stop?'

'Probably!' she laughed, hugging his arm as they started walking. 'You must be tired and hungry after that long journey. We'll go home and have something to eat.'

'Have you got to get straight back?' he queried, his face relaxing into a wide grin when she shook her head. 'Great! Where can we go for a nice quiet lunch? Somewhere we can sit and talk, just the two of us?'

'In Whinforth, we're not accustomed to going out for lunch!' she commented wryly, but indicated across the busy road. 'That little café's pleasant enough, though.'

'I was thinking about somewhere we can push the boat out, queen. Somewhere classy.'

'The Feathers,' she answered at once.

'It was a coaching inn in the olden days, and is a very nice hotel now. They put on wedding receptions and dinner dances and suchlike.'

'The Feathers it is!' Slipping an arm about her waist, he bent to plant a kiss on her forehead. 'Then afterwards, you can give me the guided tour of this old town of yours!'

Ellen had set foot inside The Feathers only once before, and that had been through the tradesmen's door. She'd been fourteen, and the Butterworths' paperboy had let them down, so Ellen had cycled across town with the hotel's newspapers and magazines.

'This is a nice place, isn't it?' remarked Brian, glancing around the dining-room as he opened the menu. 'The sort of place we'll be seeing a lot of in the years ahead.'

'Come into a fortune, have you?' she enquired, running an eye over the prices.

'Hardly! But I've enough saved to take the first steps towards making one!' he grinned, ordering white wine to accompany their meal.

'Wine too!' Ellen's eyes widened. 'In the middle of the day?'

'It has been known, queen!'

'What are you up to?' she enquired curiously, studying his confident, ebullient face across the table. 'There's definitely something different about you, Brian!'

'New shade of lipstick? Different hair-do?'

'Stop acting the goat and tell me what's going on!'

He considered her over the rim of his glass. 'Like I said in my letter, me and Nick have done a lot of talking these past months. He's helped me a lot. Shown me what I need to look out for and how to avoid the pitfalls. Put me in touch with some useful contacts.'

'You also spoke of leaving Liverpool and moving to Yorkshire,' she began. 'Are you serious about that?'

'Never more so.'

'It's a long way from the sea, Brian!

Whatever will you do up here?'

'I've got a few plans. Tell you more about them later,' he replied, pausing while the waiter served their lunch. 'I made a fair bit of money from that Lisbon trip, and Jack McBride's been very reasonable about me leaving the shipping office.'

'You're really leaving?' she echoed, taken aback. 'I thought it — '

'Might be just hot air?' he chipped in, arching an eyebrow. 'Just me shooting my big mouth off like always? Ah, don't look at me all apologetic, queen! I couldn't blame you if that's exactly what you did think! But this time it's not all talk.'

'So you really are leaving McBride's?'

'I've left,' he answered smugly, attacking his steak. 'Worked my last day.'

She stared at him, the implications of how Brian's decision would change her own life flashing across her mind. 'What happens now?'

'Plenty! And I owe a fair bit to

McBride, y'know. His missus used to tell me I reminded him of himself, when he'd been young and starting out. I reckon that's so, because he give me top-notch references and a couple of introductory letters. To the bank, among others.'

'The bank?' queried Ellen, scarcely tasting her food. Everything was happening so fast.

'New businesses need money, queen,' he answered patiently. 'With Jack McBride's name and reputation behind me, I've had no bother arranging finances. Or anything else, for that matter! I just need to nip back to Liverpool to collect my stuff. There's not much of it. I'm used to carrying all my worldly goods around in a kitbag!

'Aren't you going to congratulate me?' He poured himself another glass of wine, grinning at Ellen's bemused expression. 'I'm here to stay — if you'll have me!'

Her mind was still reeling when they emerged from The Feathers and were

223

strolling arm-in-arm around the steeply cobbled streets and narrow wynds of the old wool town. The day was cold, but crisp and bright, with winter sun gilding the grey stones of the shops and weavers' cottages, and glittering upon the clear, rushing waters of the Whin. They went down along the riverbank and Ellen hugged Brian's arm closer as they walked, the dazzling sunlight warming their chill faces. She'd wanted to ask him a hundred and one questions about his plans, but *'All in good time, queen — be patient!'* was all the reply Brian was prepared to give just now, and with that she had to be content.

She was right about Brian's being different though, considered Ellen, watching as he turned from her to gaze over the river and far away to the hills. He had changed during the months of their separation — and perhaps she'd changed too, because their reunion certainly hadn't been at all as Ellen expected.

It was late afternoon before they returned to the corner shop, turning down the ginnel and going through the yard into the kitchen where Dorothy was seated at the fireside with her knitting.

'It's smashing to meet you at last, Mrs Butterworth!' grinned Brian, taking her hand gently. 'And thanks for offering to put me up — I'll try not to be too much of a nuisance.'

'Don't be daft, lad!' returned Dorothy warmly, immediately taking a liking to her daughter's chirpy young man. 'You're family, or as near as makes no difference. Where else would you stay? Besides, it'll be grand having you here. And call me 'Dorothy', by the way.'

'Like the little girl in *The Wizard of Oz*?' he queried, eyes twinkling down at her.

'Aye, but this definitely isn't Kansas!' laughed Dorothy. 'Sit yourself down while Nellie puts the kettle on. Jen'll be through in a minute. There's a few folk in the shop just now.'

'Nellie's been showing me around the town — oh, shall I give you a push over to the table? There! How's that?' he went on, settling Dorothy at the table where Ellen was spreading a pretty floral cloth and setting out cups and saucers. 'Yeah, we went all over the place, didn't we, queen? Actually, I've decided to move up here permanent. There's nowt to keep me in Liverpool, and I like the look of your town. I'm putting my roots down right here!'

'That's wonderful news!' cried Dorothy, delighted at the prospect of her daughter and son-in-law settling close by. 'Which — oh, here's Jeanette!'

Jeanette stood framed by the curtained doorway from the shop, her huge blue eyes wide and alight as she caught sight of Brian.

'It *was* you!'

'Was it?' gasped Brian, feigning alarm. 'What have I done?'

Jeanette burst out laughing, tripping

into the kitchen and shaking her head.

'I'm not going potty after all!'

'That's certainly a comfort to know, queen!' Rising, he took a couple of strides towards her and took her hand. 'Pleased to meet you, Jeanette! Nellie's told me no end about you.'

'Good things, I hope!' she returned wryly.

'Only the very best!' His gaze held hers as he slowly released her hand.

'Yes, it *was* you!' she continued, perching on the chair next to Brian's. 'Nellie insisted it couldn't have been you, but I'd recognise you anywhere! I was coming out of the music shop on Princes Street on Monday and we almost bumped into each other. Remember?'

'Brian only arrived this morning,' put in Ellen a little irritably, carefully placing the cosy-covered teapot into the centre of the table. 'I said you were mistaken.'

However, Jeanette merely shook her head again, her eyes dancing mischievously as she contemplated her future brother-in-law. 'I saw you going into

Menzies' bank, Brian. You *were* here in Whinforth on Monday, weren't you?'

'Yeah, I was.' He shrugged, casting an apologetic glance across the table to Ellen. 'Sorry, queen. I was going to tell you all about it later. It was meant to be a surprise.'

'It's certainly proved to be that!' retorted Ellen stiffly, pouring tea. 'All the while we were walking around town this afternoon, and you never let on you'd already seen it all!'

'But I hadn't!' he insisted earnestly. 'I didn't have time to have a proper look round on Monday. I just went to the bank and a few other appointments and that was it. Honest.'

'I'm really sorry, Nellie,' murmured Jeanette, chastened by her sister's stony expression. 'Sorry, Brian. Me and my big mouth! I've completely ruined your surprise.'

'Can't be helped, queen — and I've been accused of having a big mouth myself more than once, so don't worry about it!' responded Brian easily,

228

reaching across to touch Ellen's hand. 'It's no big dark secret. I planned on telling Nellie — and the two of you — all about it tonight, anyway.'

'Even so — ' Jeanette was interrupted by the jangle of the brass bell above the shop door, and with no small measure of relief made for the curtained doorway. 'Customers! Excuse me!'

In a flash, Jeanette was gone and Ellen felt the warmth of Brian's fingertips upon her skin. Her gaze slid to their joined hands and then to Brian's face. He was smiling at her, but Ellen's heart sank. There was an emptiness deep within her, a pain so sharp it caught her breath.

For, from the moment her vivacious younger sister had appeared, Brian hadn't been able to take his eyes from Jeanette . . .

# 13

Dorothy finished chatting to the vicar as Jeanette served him with his newspaper and tobacco, and with considerable effort, pushed herself through to the kitchen where Ellen was making coffee and cutting bread for sandwiches.

'The pasties come out of the oven shortly,' remarked Dorothy. 'Don't forget to take a couple over to Brian. He'll be glad of something hot, the hours he's putting in at that draughty old shop!'

'It still needs plenty doing to it, but honestly Ma, if you'd seen how dilapidated that place was when Brian took it over!' She shook her head. 'Goodness knows how long the premises had been unoccupied!'

'Donkeys' years!' Jeanette called from the shop. 'It used to be a cobbler's. Father and son. But the son didn't come back from the war, and his parents just closed up and moved away. It's been empty ever since.'

'I have seen it — only from outside, though,' reflected Dorothy, checking on the pasties. 'Brian showed me when he took me out to get my wool the other day. I must say, it looks a canny little place. And I'm sure the neighbouring shopkeepers will be glad to have it open for business again. There's nothing brings a street down worse that a shuttered shop!'

'That's true, but is there really need for a decorators' merchant in a small town like Whinforth?' queried Ellen soberly. 'I don't recall there ever having been such a business here before.'

'Which surely increases its prospects of success!' chimed Jeanette, coming through the curtains. 'The timing is perfect, I reckon. Because Brian's right, people are beginning to titivate their homes again now, and they'll be able to buy their paint and wallpaper right here in town instead of having to travel miles away.'

'I wouldn't mind doing a bit of titivating!' commented Dorothy with a smile. 'Since you girls decorated the back parlour for me, the rest of the house looks shabby! Besides, it's not just ordinary folk Brian's shop'll cater for, is it? He'll be supplying the trade, too.'

'If everything goes according to his plans, Brian will be *part* of the trade! He served his time before the war.' Concern creased Ellen's brow. 'He sees the merchant's shop as another string to his bow when he starts up as a painter and decorator. Brian's put his heart and soul into this venture, but it's so ambitious and such an enormous risk!'

'Don't worry, Nellie. Brian won't fail. He's far too smart,' declared Jeanette confidently. 'He saw the potential and he's enterprising enough to throw everything at it. Plus, he's not afraid of hard work, and he's got bags of get-up-and-go.

'Mount Pleasant's a busy little street and the shops along there are thriving.

Kennedy's Decorators' Merchant will be a massive success,' she concluded blithely, looping an arm about her elder sister's shoulders. 'This time next year, when you and Brian are married and business is booming, you'll wonder why you were worrying — you just wait and see if I'm not right!'

Ellen was careful to conceal her misgivings when Brian greeted her at the premises on Mount Pleasant, and they were sitting together on a saw-horse, sharing the lunch she'd prepared. Looking over the rim of her cup, she took in the newly-repaired weather-tight window frames and doors, the neatly-plastered walls ready for painting, and the stack of timber Brian would transform into shelving, for he was tackling almost all of the refurbishment himself.

She tried to envisage what Brian must see in his mind's eye. He had ribbed Ellen more than once for fussing and mithering. Perhaps he — and Jeanette — were right and she *was* being overly cautious. Why shouldn't the business be a resounding success? Brian would certainly work tenaciously to make it so.

'. . . I don't want to outstay my welcome, y'see,' she realised Brian was saying as he bit into his pasty. 'Ay, these are great! Tell your Jeanette, *Ten out of ten!*' No, like I was saying . . . it's been great of your mam to put me up all this while, but I reckon it's time I started looking for digs. Or better still, somewhere proper for us to live after we're wed.'

'Ma's pleased you're staying with us,' replied Ellen, finishing her coffee. 'You're family. She'd be hurt if you moved out. Besides, lodgings aren't cheap. Not even in a small town like Whinforth. At least have a word with Ma before you make any decisions.'

'Yeah, of course. And, talking of decisions, the hairdresser's two doors up have made their minds up. They've agreed my price and asked me to get on with it!'

'You're doing all their redecorating?' exclaimed Ellen, thrilled. 'That's wonderful, Brian!'

'First of many, queen! Make a good job of this one, and word will spread around town like wildfire — hairdressers' are proper gossip shops!'

'Why didn't you tell me your news when I first came in?' she queried in wonder. 'How could you keep something like that to yourself — no, don't tell me. It was a surprise!'

'Got it in one!' he guffawed. 'I was planning on taking you out for a nice meal at The Feathers to celebrate. It may be my last evening off for a bit. I can only work at the hairdresser's after they close, and because everything has to be dry and my stuff cleared away before they open again in the morning, there's a serious limit on what I can do each night. It's going to be a long job.'

'I'm so proud of you, Brian!' she beamed. 'This is a grand start.'

'A pretty profitable one, too.' He grinned broadly, taking her hand and bringing it to his lips. 'We have to start making plans for our future, queen!'

' . . . I'll be glad to do the stairs and landing, Dot,' Brian was saying. He was sitting in the kitchen, arms out-stretched, while Dorothy wound the skein of wool looped about his wrists into a neat ball. 'Since I've been working at the hairdresser's, I'm start-ing to get my eye in again. I'll fetch some colour charts and pattern books so you can pick your paint and paper.'

'Are you sure you don't mind?' she queried, looking at him over the rim of her new specs. 'You've not got much time for yourself as it is, what with doing up your own shop and working at the hairdresser's.'

'Ah, no worries!' He grinned, going on seriously: 'But are you sure, about me staying on here? I can afford digs now, y'know.'

'And waste your hard-earned brass lining a greedy landlord's pockets?' she exclaimed in disgust. 'You save your money, lad! You're welcome here for as long as you like, and that goes for after you're wed too. Oh, I know young couples want a place of their own, but nothing'd make me happier than for you and Nellie to live here until you get on your feet and find somewhere nice — '

Dorothy suddenly broke off, straining her ears to catch what was going on in the shop.

'They're saying something about Ada — take me through, Brian. Quick!'

Alex Munro was in the shop, with Peggy and Robbie standing silent and wide-eyed at his side.

'We never see you in here at this hour, Mr Munro,' began Dorothy at once. 'It's Ada brings the bairns in on their way to school. What's wrong?'

'Mrs Heggie went over on her gammy ankle, Ma!' It was Jeanette who replied. 'Alex was just telling us.'

'How is she?' asked Dorothy, her voice sharp with concern. 'What happened?'

'Mrs Heggie caught her footing on

the uneven cobbles near the bridge last evening. She's badly twisted her ankle and fractured her wrist. Doctor Irwin has prescribed something to ease the pain, and for shock. Mrs Heggie was very shaken by the accident, but she's comfortable and resting at home now,' reassured Alex.

'Dear Lord!' Dorothy's thin fingers fussed with the amber glass brooch pinned at the neck of her blouse. 'Poor Ada. She's always been frightened of tripping, ever since that fall she had years ago. If there's anything we can do, Mr Munro — keep an eye on the bairns, maybe, while you're at the office — You've only got to say. You know that?'

'Thank you, Mrs Butterworth.' He smiled, glancing over at Ellen as she silently pressed a little cone of sweets into each child's hand. 'You're very kind.'

'Mr Munro!' Ellen called after him as he made to leave. 'Ada's at home, you said? Would it be alright if I visited her?

In case she needs anything?'

'She'll be delighted to see you, I'm sure.' Turning back, Alex reached into the inside pocket of his overcoat. 'This is the key to the front door — I have a spare at the office — just let yourself in. Mrs Heggie's in the kitchen. You recall where it is?'

'At the end of the hall.' She nodded, taking the key.

Alex's gaze moved across to Dorothy, and he smiled ruefully. 'Mrs Heggie was concerned about letting you down. She told me you'd arranged to go to the cinema today.'

'Tell her Bette Davis can wait another week or two!' Dorothy responded, raising a hand and waving to the children as the family quit the shop.

The door had no sooner closed than it jangled open again, and for the next hour or so there was a steady stream of customers.

'I'd like to go and see Ada,' began Ellen, when finally there were a few quiet moments.

'I'd like to go myself, if I could!' returned Dorothy, banging the arm of the wheelchair with the flat of her hand in vexation. 'You get yourself up there, Nellie.'

'I'll just hang on here until it slackens off,' Ellen said, as the door opened again. 'We're really busy today.'

'No, go straight away,' argued Dorothy. 'I don't like thinking of Ada all alone up there at Lane End House. I can give Jeanette a hand.'

'And what about me?' chipped in Brian breezily, sticking his head through the curtained doorway. 'I'm not just a pretty face, y'know! You get on your way, queen. I'll man the counter with these good ladies!'

'You'll be going to work on your own shop soon!'

'The dry rot'll still be there tomorrow,' he countered. 'And one of the perks of being your own boss is choosing your own hours!'

'But — '

'Not another word!' he declared,

yanking her through to the kitchen. 'Handling customers is good practice for when I open my own place, and I've got your mam and sister to whip me into shape. You get yourself off to see the old girl, and don't hurry back. Take as much time as you need.

'Right, Miss Jeanette,' went on Brian enthusiastically, diving past the curtain into the shop. 'Point me to my pinny and tell me what to do!'

Dorothy followed Ellen into the kitchen. 'Here, Nellie. Take these. It's *The People's Friend* that Ada would've collected this morning, and a little box of chocolates. She'll need a bit of a pick-me-up. And don't fret about being away from the shop. Brian's right. Between us, we'll manage fine — are you alright?' She paused, considering her elder daughter's pale face. 'You're looking right peaky!'

'Haven't been sleeping too well,' she answered truthfully, forcing a smile as she fetched her coat and hat. 'I've got a few things on my mind.'

Dorothy's eyes crinkled as she smiled knowingly. 'From what Brian's been saying lately, I reckon the pair of you have quite a lot of things on your minds! Be sure to give Ada our love, and do all you can to help her, pet.'

★ ★ ★

'Ada! It's Ellen,' she called softly, opening the front door at Lane End House. 'Are you in the kitchen?'

'Aye, come on through!'

The wireless was mumbling quietly from a shelf in the corner and Ada was seated at the fireside, her chair plump with cushions and her heavily-strapped ankle upon a padded stool. Her right wrist and lower arm, thickly encased in a plaster cast, was supported by a sling.

'By, you're a sight for sore eyes!' the elderly woman beamed. 'I wasn't expecting a visitor!'

'Even better than that, I bear gifts!' laughed Ellen, unpacking her basket. 'And I have strict instructions not to rush back to the shop — so you're stuck with me for a fair while. How about a fresh pot of tea?'

'Lovely!'

'Something to eat?'

Ada shook her head. 'Mr Munro made porridge for breakfast. Bless him, he did his best, but it certainly stuck to your ribs!'

'To the pots, too!' Ellen observed, glancing at the heap of dishes in the sink. 'While the kettle's boiling, I'll get these washed and put away.'

'It was the daftest thing,' remarked Ada, glowering at her arm and ankle. 'I was coming home from church last night. I'd just crossed the bridge when I caught my shoe against them cobbles at the bottom. This wonky foot of mine just gave way and down I went. Must've put my hand out to save myself and did this!' she finished in disgust.

'It could've been a lot worse, Ada,' commented Ellen sympathetically. 'However did you manage to get home?'

'Hanging onto walls and hedges like

a drunken sailor!' she grinned. 'So here I am. Laid up and good for nothing.'

'Make the most of the rest while you can!' cautioned Ellen, adding a little more coal and wood to the fire.

'Queer thing is, it's not my foot that's the most bother,' went on Ada. 'With the stick, I can drag myself about a bit. But not having my right hand is a real pig! It took me half an hour to put on my stockings this morning — never seen such a palaver!'

'You're going to be ham-fisted for a fair while, that's for sure.' Ellen remarked thoughtfully, finding the biscuit barrel and bringing the tea tray over to the fireside. 'But if we get ourselves organised and you tell me what needs doing, we should manage alright.'

'Oh, no.' Ada shook her head firmly. 'It's grand of you to offer, Nellie, but you've your own job to do. That's the reason you come back to Whinforth in the first place!'

'The situation's much improved now,

thank heavens,' she replied. 'Brian's helping Jeanette, and although Ma still tires easily, she enjoys nothing better than taking a turn behind the counter.'

'You'd need to shoot your ma to keep her out of that shop,' agreed Ada sagely. 'It weren't the same without her, neither.'

'No, it wasn't,' murmured Ellen, going on with a smile: 'Suppose I make a start with the cleaning? I fetched bread and milk on my way up here, but I'll go shopping later and prepare an evening meal that you'll only need to put a light under. Mr Munro can dish up when he gets home. You mustn't attempt lifting hot pans and dishes left-handed.'

'Are you sure about this, Nellie?' persisted Ada doubtfully. 'Can they really spare you at home?'

'They won't even notice I'm gone!' Ellen quipped lightly, but her eyes were downcast as the laughter and banter filling the shop when she'd left it rang again in her ears. 'I must let Mr Munro know what we're doing too, and that I'll collect Peggy and Robbie from school this afternoon.'

'He'll be obliged for that, because I know for a fact he has some sort of important meeting with a client today,' said Ada. 'There's a telephone here. You can telephone him at the office.'

Ellen considered. 'I'd rather not interrupt him at his work, especially if it might be a bad time. No, I'll pop down to his office and leave a note with the clerk. He can pass it on to Mr Munro without causing any disturbance.'

Later that morning, Ellen made her way to the premises of Messrs Swanson, Newell and Munro, attorneys at law, situated midway along the winding lane tucked behind St. Bede's in Church Mews. She'd never before paid much attention to the small-windowed, sturdy stone buildings, and it wasn't until she pushed open the narrow oak door and stepped down into a stone-flagged, dimly-lit room that Ellen realised how very old the place must be.

She was explaining her mission to an elderly clerk, who'd emerged like a wraith from the shadows, when an inner door opened and Alex Munro appeared.

'Miss Butterworth! I thought I recognised your voice,' he greeted her pleasantly. 'Can I be of help?'

'I was about to leave this message with your clerk, Mr Munro.'

He took the envelope, smiling at her over the tops of his spectacles and indicating his office. 'Have you time to wait while I read it?'

Ellen nodded, entering the small office. It was dark and cramped, its walls lined by shelves heaped with musty old books and bundles of faded, dog-eared papers. A fire burned in the grate and the small window with its tiny square panes was pushed open, admitting the sounds of voices, horses and hoofs from the walled yard beyond.

'It is quite an interesting place, isn't it?' remarked Alex, glancing up from reading her note and smiling. Ellen blushed slightly, unaware she'd been staring at her surroundings. 'Apparently, a couple of centuries ago, these premises were a clergyman's residence that doubled as Whinforth's court-house. Trials, inquests, suits and all manner of legal proceedings were heard in the rooms upstairs.

'Please, won't you take a seat?' he went on. 'Can I offer you tea? I was just about to send for some.'

'That would be nice, thank you,' she answered, looking around the room again and smiling. 'I'd never given any thought to what the Mews was like in olden times, and certainly hadn't guessed at its colourful past!'

'A frequently notorious past too, as contemporary documents illustrate only too vividly!' he grinned, waving an arm to the laden shelves and cupboards. 'The Law hoards papers!'

'So I see!' she laughed as a tray was brought in and Alex Munro poured their tea. 'Will it be alright if I lend Ada a little help for a while? I thought I might do some shopping and then collect Peggy and Robbie from school.'

'That would be marvellous, Miss Butterworth!' he replied emphatically. 'It's very generous of you to offer; however, I'm aware of your responsibilities at home and — '

'Once Ada and I get organised, I'll only be from the shop for a few hours at a time, and my fiancé's lending a hand while I'm away,' she interrupted quietly. 'It won't be any trouble at all.'

'If you're sure.' He smiled, his earnest eyes warm. 'Thank you very much indeed, Miss Butterworth. I often have to work long hours here, and was particularly concerned about upsetting Peggy and Robbie's routine.'

'Don't worry, Mr Munro, we'll manage just fine,' she assured him, her gaze suddenly lighting upon a bundle of sheet music balancing on the corner of his cluttered desk. 'Oh, this looks familiar! It's the duet you and Jeanette are doing, isn't it?'

'Guilty as charged!' he replied ruefully. 'Whenever I have a spare moment,

I study all the music from the show — although, to the great relief of everyone here, I haven't yet burst into song during office hours! Do you read music yourself?'

'Not very well, but we've all been helping Jeanette learn her songs,' answered Ellen. 'I've missed the last couple of Players meetings, but Jeanette tells me that after the show runs at the school for three nights, you'll be giving performances at the Infirmary and over at the servicemen's nursing home in Gylbeck?'

'Yes, we're going on the road,' he agreed solemnly, but it seemed to Ellen there was a twinkle of humour in Alex's Munro's clever grey eyes. 'Just like Bob Hope and Bing Crosby.'

★   ★   ★

'Hey, Nellie!' cried Jeanette one afternoon, when Ellen was collecting the children's story papers and Ada's *Family Star* before setting off for Lane

End House. 'You're humming my tune!'

'Was I?' she murmured. 'I hadn't even realised!'

'I'm surprised we're not *all* humming it!' returned Brian, looking very at home behind the counter and weighing out lemon drops for Beattie Clough from next door. 'We've heard you rehearsing it so often, we're brainwashed! I hear it in my sleep.'

Jeanette planted her hands on her hips. 'I do hope you're not complaining about my voice, Brian Kennedy!'

'Would I dare?' he countered, winking at Beattie Clough. 'Here's your sweets, Mrs Clough. And an ounce of thick Virginia twist, wasn't it?'

Ellen methodically checked the contents of her basket before leaving, making sure she had the library books Ada had asked her to borrow. 'Jen, when I get back this evening, we'll cut out your dress if you've decided which pattern you want.'

'I have — well, almost!' declared the

younger woman exuberantly. 'At least, I've narrowed it down to three styles. With a definite leaning towards the sleeveless one with the bolero!'

'That's . . . promising,' responded Ellen, with an affectionate smile to her vivacious sister. 'Whatever you choose, Jen, you'll look stunning on the night! See you later, everyone!'

'Supper's nearly ready, Peggy!' Ellen popped her head into the sitting-room, where the little girl was sitting beside the window as usual, school books spread over the table before her. 'How are you getting on?'

'Not very well,' she sighed, pushing one of her heavy braids back over her shoulder. 'I just can't get the last bit right, Miss Ellie.'

'What is it you're doing?' She drew out one of the straight-backed chairs and sat down. 'Hmm. Geography. I can remember having problems with that, too. Which part are you stuck on?'

'I've answered all the questions except number eight,' explained Peggy, pointing out a paragraph in a well-worn textbook. 'I think I've drawn the map alright, but I can't get my answer to say what I want to say.'

'Tricky, isn't it?' considered Ellen, bowing her head over the books. 'I know! Why don't you just tell me everything you want to say, and then we'll try to work out how to write it down . . . ?'

Engrossed in the problematic task, it wasn't until Robbie burst into the sitting-room that the pair looked up from the books.

'What are you doing?' he demanded indignantly. 'Mrs Heggie sent me to fetch you. She said if you don't come right now and eat your supper, she'll put it out for my hedgehog!'

★ ★ ★

They were such good children.

Each evening, Peggy helped Ellen get Robbie ready for bed; and most evenings, they'd have to hunt high and low for Little Bear, without whom Robbie couldn't fall asleep. However, as Peggy pointed out, the threadbare old toy was always in one of half a dozen places, so it usually didn't take too long to find him.

'Although,' she added soberly, surveying Ellen through her round glasses, 'I can't fathom why Robbie keeps losing him!'

Peggy was grown-up beyond her eight years, but that was hardly surprising. She was very responsible too, watching over her small brother like a mother and taking an interest in the running of the house.

'Father won't be home until very late,' she whispered one night, after Robbie had fallen asleep while Ellen was reading the story. 'He's having dinner with one of old Mr Swanson's very rich clients. The Colonel has a dispute about mining rights on some of his land.'

'Your father mentioned he often has to work late.'

'He often has to visit places far away,

too. He goes all the way to York and Harrogate. Even Scarborough, sometimes,' continued Peggy, finishing her cocoa and reaching into the drawer of her bedside cabinet. 'Miss Ellie, a few days ago you told me you were going to help your sister make a new dress for the show she and Father are singing in together. I — I made this for you in my needlework class.'

'Oh, Peggy — it's beautiful!' cried Ellen, taking the neatly-sewn little case with its embroidered cross-stitch edging and daisy motif. 'Fancy your making me a present!'

'It's for your needles, see?' Her small fingers opened up the case, revealing the felt leaves within. 'It fastens with the little bow.'

'It's the nicest present I've ever been given, Peggy,' Ellen murmured, a lump coming to her throat as she gazed down into the wide grey eyes and bent to lightly kiss the child's soft hair. 'I'll treasure this always, love!'

With the precious sewing case safely

tucked inside her handbag, Ellen strode home with a spring in her step, and felt in fine spirits when she let herself into the yard. Jeanette's crystal-clear voice floating upon the piano's mellow notes was drifting from the parlour. Ellen was aware how very nervous her sister was about singing in the show, but she had absolutely no cause to be. Jeanette was wonderful.

She paused unseen in the doorway to listen. The parlour was bright and cheery as usual, with everyone gathered about the old upright piano. Dorothy's thin fingers were coaxing a sweeping melody from the smooth keys as Jeanette launched into the duet she was to sing with Alex Munro.

*'You'll never know just how much
  I love you,
You'll never know just how much I
  care . . . '*

Brian's voice suddenly joined hers, and Ellen realised she'd never heard

steaming copper with huge wooden tongs. 'Perm?'

'I'd like summat a bit different.' Dorothy wheeled herself out into the stone-flagged wash-house adjoining the kitchen. 'I've never been to this salon of course, it's usually too dear, but I've found no matter what you ask for, you end up with whatever the hairdresser wants to give you.'

'There's a huge photo of Elizabeth Taylor in the salon's window, Ma. Perhaps you'll come out looking like her!'

'I'd pay full price for that!' she laughed, going on: 'Brian was telling me it'll not be long before he's ready to open up the merchant. I'm a bit surprised you and him haven't made any wedding plans, Nellie. I'd save my cheap hair-do, if I knew the date.'

'Nice try, Ma!' remarked Ellen, hefting the wet washing out into the yard and gratefully setting it down beside the mangle. 'But I'd stick to your plan of having it done for Jen's show!'

'Ah, fair enough!' chuckled Dorothy,

pushing close to the mangle and easing the lumpy corner of a sheet through the rollers as Ellen cranked the great handle. 'I don't suppose the pair of you have had much chance for making arrangements. You're both so busy just now.'

'I know I've been spending quite a lot of time up at Lane End House,' began Ellen breathlessly, pausing from turning the great handle, 'but — '

'You're needed up there, Nellie.' interrupted Dorothy. 'Ada can't be expected to cook and clean and take care of two bairns with her right hand in a sling! With all of us fitting in with each other and working together, everything's going along like clockwork here, so don't you fret about spending time away from the shop!

'I'm enjoying being back behind the counter for a few hours. Doing a bit of serving and chatting to my customers. I feel like I'm alive again,' she concluded, adding with concern: 'What about yourself, though? You're looking pale, Nellie. Are you sure you're not doing too much? It's a fair trek back and forth to Lane End House twice a day, and that's without the work you do when you get there.'

'It's no bother at all, Ma,' she reassured her, her eyes lowered to the task of mangling sheets. 'Peggy and Robbie are smashing children, and Ada and I work well together. I'm quite enjoying it. There, that's the last of the sheets!'

'While you get them pegged out,' Dorothy reached down into the bucket, 'I'll fold these towels ready for mangling.'

The laundry was hanging limply across lines strung the length of the yard when Brian came in through the ginnel door, ducking beneath the wet washing and letting himself into the kitchen.

'I've just taken on my first employee!' he announced to nobody in particular, since the room was quite empty.

'There'll be no stopping you now, lad!' called Dorothy from the shop. 'We're in here! Come and tell us all about it!'

'Better still,' he replied, taking off his coat and tossing it over a chair back, 'I'll make us a brew first to go with these cream cakes I've just bought!'

'Spill the beans!' demanded Jeanette five minutes later, when Brian emerged through the curtain with a tray of tea and cakes for them all.

'Where's Nellie?' he asked, looking around in consternation. 'I thought she was in here. I made her a cuppa!'

'Ah, you've just missed her!' replied Dorothy ruefully. 'She went a bit early because she had a few things to do before collecting the bairns from school. It's the little lad's birthday today.'

'Oh, blast! That's right!' Brian slapped his forehead with the heel of his hand. 'She told me this morning she'd be going early, and probably be back later than usual — I clean forgot.'

'What about this employee of yours?' prompted Jeanette impatiently, sipping the hot tea. 'The first of many, I presume!'

'Certainly hope so, queen!' grinned

Brian, setting down his cup to serve a woman with hairgrips and Woodbines. 'I'm paying him by the hour until the merchant opens up. Then he'll be on full wages. Meanwhile, he's helping me finish the place off. A lot of the work, putting up the shelves and fittings and such, is two-man jobs.'

'What's his name? Do we know him? What's he like?' quizzed Jeanette. 'Young? Old? Good-looking?'

'Arthur's a willing worker, that's all I'm bothered about. You'll have to make your own mind up about whether he's good-looking!' replied Brian, an irrepressible grin spreading across his face. 'Actually, Arthur'll be running the merchant because ... *I've* landed another decorating job! Four old mill cottages on the edge of town. The details aren't quite nailed down yet, but as good as!'

'Well done, lad!' beamed Dorothy, raising her tea cup in toast. 'Every success to you — you deserve it!'

'Hear, hear!' chimed Jeanette, her

cheeks pink. 'Wait until you tell Nellie! She's already ever so proud of you, Brian. She'll be thrilled to bits with this news!'

★ ★ ★

Ellen bustled the Munro children through the town from school and over the drovers' bridge towards the comfortable houses and neat gardens stretching away along the bank following the bend of the river.

When they turned the corner and Lane End House appeared below them, Ellen held both arms out wide from her sides.

'Are we ready?' she asked, just as she'd done every afternoon since she'd been collecting Peggy and Robbie from school. 'Are we really ready?'

Each child nodded, clasping one of Ellen's hands.

'Wheeeeeeee!' cried the three together, running for all they were worth down the lane towards the red-brick house.

Breaking free from Ellen's grasp, Robbie flew like the wind to the gate.

'I won, Miss Ellie!' he whooped. 'I won! I won!'

'You were so fast!' laughed Ellen, opening up the front door. 'Mmm, something smells good — wonder what Mrs Heggie's baking for you?'

'Hope it's gingerbread men!' Robbie clattered down the hallway and around into the kitchen. 'Mrs Heggie! I beat Peggy and Miss Ellie to the gate and — '

The kitchen door banged shut behind him and Ellen and Peggy stood in the hallway taking off their coats.

'You made the gingerbread, didn't you?' Peggy's wide grey eyes looked up at Ellen through the round spectacles. 'Mrs Heggie can't stir things or roll them out since she hurt her wrist.'

'I helped with the stirring and rolling,' replied Ellen. 'But I followed Mrs Heggie's recipe carefully and she told me what to do.'

Peggy nodded soberly. 'Mrs Heggie's

teaching me how to bake, too. I'm going to make black bun for Father one day. Black bun's his favourite.'

Ellen thought a moment. 'I don't think I've ever tasted black bun. What's it like, Peggy?'

'Oh, it's very tasty! It's sort of a big round cake. Full of currants and sultanas and spices.'

'It sounds delicious! Will you teach me to make it one day?'

'I'd like that,' smiled the little girl, retying the loose ribbon on one of her braids and adding in a whisper, 'I let Robbie win today, Miss Ellie. Because it's his birthday — but don't tell him, will you?'

'It'll be our secret, Peggy!' she replied as the small girl picked up her satchel and started into the sitting room. 'Aren't you going to get some gingerbread, too?'

'I've homework.' She set her bulging satchel onto the table beside the window. 'Do you think Father will come home early tonight? He said he'd try, but . . . '

'I'm sure he'll be here just as soon as he can, pet.'

Peggy nodded, her head immediately bowed over her arithmetic books.

'I'll fetch some cocoa and ginger-bread to keep you going while you work,' said Ellen cheerfully, going from the room and knowing Peggy would keep watch from the window for Alex Munro's spare frame appearing around the corner of the gate.

'If I had a silver threepence,' tutted Ada, hooking her stick onto the corner of the kitchen cabinet while she used her left hand to deftly slide gingerbread men onto the cooling rack, 'for every meal I've cooked for Mr Munro that's dried up because he's been kept late at that blessed office!'

'He does seem to work long hours,' commented Ellen, fetching the cocoa tin. 'And do a fair bit of travelling about visiting clients.'

'He's in court sometimes, and all.' Ada bobbed her chin. 'Course, with Mr Munro being the youngest partner in the firm, the old pair leave him to do all the traipsing about the county while they stay put! I just hope he manages to get here at a decent hour for his boy's birthday tea.'

'There's still plenty of time,' replied Ellen optimistically, pouring the cocoa. 'Where's Robbie now?'

'Feeding the birds.'

'He'll be there a while. I'll take his cocoa and gingerbread out to him,' said Ellen, fetching a bowl of scraps from the pantry. 'Is there anything else for his hedgehog . . . ?'

Robbie was sitting on the little steps that led down into the large garden, his arms wrapped about his legs and his chin resting on his knees. Ellen crept out very slowly so as not to disturb the birds darting back and forth from the bird table, and crouched beside him.

'Brought food and water for your hedgehog,' she whispered, setting down his cocoa and plate. 'And something for you too!'

He nodded, never taking his eyes

from the hungry robins and sparrows and starlings as he reached for a gingerbread man and bit into it. 'Mrs Tiggywinkle doesn't come until after dark,' he murmured, nodding towards a thick gorse bush. 'That's her water bowl under there. Some people give hedgehogs milk, you know. But Father says that's bad for them. Water's best.'

'I'm sure he's right. I've never seen a hedgehog properly.'

'They only come out at night,' replied Robbie, inching out a hand for his cocoa. 'Sometimes, Father lets me stay up and sit in the window so I can see Mrs Tiggywinkle. She's only been awake a wee while. After her winter sleep, you know?'

'Ah,' replied Ellen. They sat in companionable silence a little longer before she tiptoed away with the empty dishes.

It was a couple of hours later, as Ellen and Ada were putting the finishing touches to the tea table, that Peggy's whoop of delight heralded Alex Munro's homecoming.

'Won't you please stay for supper, Miss Butterworth?' he asked quietly, standing in the hallway removing his overcoat and hat as the children danced about him. 'In honour of Robbie's birthday?'

It was a delicious meal, rounded off by Robbie's favourite raspberry jam roly-poly with lashings of thick, creamy custard and a light sponge cake topped with soft icing and six little candles. Afterwards, they gathered in the sitting-room to play Snap! and Snakes and Ladders until bedtime.

When both children were settled for the night and Alex was reading to them, the two women finished tidying the kitchen and Ellen made ready to leave, calling up the stairs as she went out into the hall.

'I'm just off! Thank you for a lovely evening — and happy birthday again, Robbie!'

'Miss Butterworth!' Alex appeared on the landing, looking down at her over the banister. 'Could you wait a moment, please?'

She nodded, smiling up at him as she pinned on her hat.

'Miss Butterworth, I've wanted to speak to you for some while, but there never seems an opportunity,' he began quietly, coming downstairs and standing beside her. 'It's, well, it's simply that I've never actually thanked you properly for all you're doing here. Nor for the great care and attention you give Peggy and Robbie. We couldn't have managed without you.'

'It's my pleasure,' she responded sincerely. 'They're lovely children and it's such fun being with them!'

'They're certainly devoted to you!' He returned her smile, continuing hesitantly, 'Actually, I was hoping you might be able to suggest a special outing for them. There wasn't much play in my own childhood, and I'm rather at a loss when it comes to planning treats. School holidays aren't far off, and I want to do something Peggy and Robbie will really enjoy.'

'They enjoyed this evening enormously,' she replied at once, adding gently: 'It's being with *you* that makes them happy, Mr Munro!'

'Well, I want to take them out as a kind of extra birthday present,' he went on soberly. 'Do you have any ideas what they might like? Or should I just ask them where they want to go?'

'You could, but a surprise is much more fun,' pondered Ellen, thinking back over conversations she'd had with the brother and sister. 'Peggy's keen to go hiking along the river, but better wait until the weather's warmer for that . . . Ah! Robbie mentioned some of his school pals have been to see *Snow White and the Seven Dwarfs*. He seemed very keen on that!'

Alex looked blank. 'The fairy tale?'

'It's a Walt Disney film, Mr Munro. Absolutely beautiful. It's in Technicolor, and filled with songs and laughter and adventure,' explained Ellen enthusiastically. 'My friend Hilary and I saw it during the war. It's intended for children, of course, but it's happy and hopeful and we loved it! I'm sure Peggy and Robbie would, too.'

'And it's on here in town? Yes, that sounds perfect.' He paused as if about to say something more, but then merely helped Ellen on with her coat and accompanied her to the front door.

Alex Munro thanked her again and bid Ellen goodnight, remaining in the chill spring air to watch her out of sight.

★   ★   ★

It was nearly a whole month since Brian had opened the doors of his shop and set up in business as a jobbing painter and decorator, and less than a week until the opening night of Jeanette's show. The whole household seemed in a flurry of nerves and excitement, but it was the letter from Hilary burning a hole in Ellen's handbag that sent her scurrying across town into Mount Pleasant to share the wonderful news with Brian.

'The boss is in the yard, miss,' explained Arthur when she entered the Decorator's Merchant. 'Shall I fetch him?'

'No, that's alright, Arthur,' she smiled, squeezing past the rough little counter. 'I'll go through!'

'Hello, queen!' beamed Brian, straightening up from loading cans of paint, bundles of dust sheets and his canvas bag of brushes and scrapers onto the handcart, alongside three sets of ladders. 'This is a nice surprise!'

'Looks like I only just caught you!' she laughed as he strode across to hug and kiss her in the privacy of the cluttered yard.

'Yeah, I'm all set to start on the weavers' cottages,' Brian replied with satisfaction. 'The landlord let them fall into disrepair during the war, of course, but now people are starting to buy houses again, he's bumped out his tenants, had the properties renovated and wants them doing up nice and modern so he can sell the lot and make a killing — what?' he broke off, looking at her suspiciously. 'You're not hearing a word I'm saying, are you?'

'It's Hilary!' cried Ellen in delight. 'She and Nick are getting married!'

'Oh, is that all?' He gave an exaggerated sigh of indifference. 'Nah, it's great news, queen.'

'It will be a very quiet wedding, in the village where Nick's family live,' went on Ellen. 'Hilary's asked me to be matron of honour! Do you suppose Nick will ask you to be his best man?'

'Doubt it,' answered Brian, bending to resume loading the handcart. 'He's got a brother. Anyhow, Nick and me were never that pally. I mean, he gave me a lot of good advice about starting up a business, and I was really grateful for his know-how, but we weren't proper mates. Not like me and Rodge.'

'You will come to the wedding, though?'

He pulled a doubtful face. 'I dunno, queen. It'll depend when it is and how busy I am here. When you're your own boss, the business always has to come first. But you'll be alright going on your own, won't you?'

'Hilary's leaving the insurance company,' Ellen continued, a little deflated as she slipped the letter back into her handbag. 'When she's worked her notice, she's coming up to Whinforth for a visit.'

'That'll be nice,' he grunted, manoeuvring a step-ladder onto the cart. 'Pass us that bottle of turps, will you, queen? Just behind you, on the window ledge.'

'I've made appointments for Ma and Jeanette to get their hair done.' She handed him the grimy bottle. 'You did a beautiful job at the salon. It looks very chic.'

'I was pleased with it — more to the point, so were they!'

'Brian, I've been thinking about the opening night of the show,' she began slowly. 'It's the first proper night out Ma's had since she was ill, and Ada and me were talking about it; and, well, I know she'd like to go too, but she'll be minding Peggy and Robbie because, of course, Mr Munro is in the show. What do you think about my offering to babysit so Ma and Ada can go to Jeanette's opening night together?'

'Sounds a great idea to me,' he returned, wedging some of the paint cans a bit more securely on the back of the cart.

'You must still go, though,' she went on. 'I wouldn't want you to miss it.'

'I'm locked into it anyway, queen.' He took his coat from where it was slung across the shafts and checked the pockets. 'I promised Jeanette I'd sort out a taxi for her and your mam. We can tie Ada onto the running board.'

Ellen reached out and covered his paint-spattered hand with her own. 'We'd planned to go together, Brian. You're sure you don't mind my crying off?'

'Positive!' He turned, giving Ellen his full attention. 'We'll go to the Saturday night show instead, just the two of us! It'll be much better for sitting in the dark listening to lovey-dovey songs . . . '

'What time did you say the taxi'll be here, Nellie?' Ada called down from her room at Lane End House. 'Do you know, I've no idea where I've put my scarf with the roses on!'

'It's not coming till half-past, so you've plenty of time,' Ellen replied, popping her head around the foot of the stairs and noticing a neatly-folded square of silk on the hall table. 'Your scarf's down here — your gloves as well!'

'By, it's so long since I've been out anywhere,' puffed Ada, coming carefully downstairs with the aid of her stick. 'I'm all in a flap!'

'You look lovely,' smiled Ellen, gazing up at her. 'That colour really suits you. I've made some tea, so all you need to do now is sit down and catch your breath till Brian and the others get here.'

Ellen had no sooner seen Ada safely into the taxi with Brian, Dorothy and

Jeanette when, from her perch at the sitting-room window, Peggy announced she'd spotted her father striding along the lane towards the gate.

'I managed to get away from the office promptly, for once!' he said, hanging his coat, hat and umbrella on the hall stand and coming down into the kitchen, where Ellen was checking the progress of the children's supper. He withdrew a compact, well-read volume from his briefcase. 'Thank you so much for letting me borrow this, Miss Butterworth. It's a delightfully-written little book, and taught me a great deal about the country-side surrounding Whinforth, as well as the plant and wildlife to be found there.'

'I hope you didn't mind my suggest-ing you read it,' she began, stirring the rice pudding before sliding it back into the electric oven. 'But when we're walking to and from school along the river bank, Peggy often asks about the different trees and flowers, and of course Robbie is constantly watching birds and looking out for any little animals.'

'I do want to encourage their interest in the natural world; but, despite having lived here since before Robbie was born, I'm ashamed to admit to having done little walking in the hills and woods, or even along the riverbank!'

'It's always easy to overlook what's right on our doorstep!' She smiled up at him, adding practically: 'Besides, your work does keep you very busy.'

'Even so. The days are lengthening now and the weather becoming warmer; I intend on making time to take the children out into the fresh air for walks and a little nature-spotting.'

'You'll enjoy it enormously! I haven't walked for many years, but when I was little, my dad and I used to go rambling every Sunday after church. He'd carried that book in his rucksack for as long as I could remember; then, when I was about Peggy's age, he gave it to me together with a battered pair of field glasses he'd brought home from France in 1918!' she related affectionately. 'We'd cross the Whin and walk the Dow Hills, down through the woods, and back over the river and along the bank into town.

'They were such happy days! Please do keep the book, Mr Munro, for Peggy and Robbie.'

'That's incredibly kind, but I can't possibly accept,' he protested quietly, his gaze falling to the worn little book in his hands. 'This book holds such dear memories, you must cherish it deeply.'

'I do, but I'd still like Peggy and Robbie to have it,' she replied simply. 'That book's packed with illustrations and information about the birds, animals, trees, rocks, hills, woods and river of Whinforth — but it's stood untouched on the shelf in Ma's parlour since before I left school and went away to secretarial college!

'Please keep it, and use it well on your walks with the children,' concluded Ellen softly. 'My dad liked things to be used, and he'd like his little book to be passed along to the next generation.'

★ ★ ★

Lane End House seemed peculiarly empty without the presence of Ada and Alex Munro and the muted mumblings of the Home Service on the sitting-room wireless.

'Didn't Father look handsome when he went off to the show, Miss Ellie?' remarked Peggy at bedtime, when they were hunting in the cupboard under the stairs for Little Bear. 'Just like Fred Astaire, I thought!'

Ellen sat back on her heels and considered. Alex Munro *had* looked surprisingly debonair when he'd come hurrying downstairs in white tie and tails, fumbling to fix a rosebud into his lapel. 'Mmm, I'd say more like Stuart Grainger myself — but you're right, Peggy, your dad did look extremely handsome!'

'I wish we could have gone to the show!' said Peggy, deftly retrieving Little Bear from behind the dustpan and brush. 'Imagine seeing all the fancy dresses and hearing all the songs!'

'I'm sure your father will take lots of photographs, as he did at the play,' replied Ellen thoughtfully. 'As for the music . . . when you're both in bed, before I read your story, why don't we have a sing-song of our own?'

After the excitement of the singing, it was a little later than usual when Peggy, as well as Robbie, fell asleep while Ellen was reading that night's chapter of *Five Go To Smuggler's Top*. Tiptoeing downstairs, she prepared a light supper for Alex Munro — who'd told her he wouldn't be joining the other Players at the coffee-house after the curtain came down — and was just putting oatcakes and the makings of cocoa onto a tray for Ada when she heard the thrum of the taxi-cab.

'Was it a good night?' she asked, opening the front door noiselessly as

Ada and Brian came up the path.

'Heaven! Your Jeanette was breathtaking. Such a pretty girl, and a voice like an angel!' whispered Ada, taking off her hat and coat. 'Brian told me the pair of you are going to see the show on Saturday night — you'll love it, Nellie! It's just grand!

'You get yourself off home now,' she went on. 'Thanks for minding the bairns — and letting me borrow your young man!'

'Hey, it was my pleasure, queen!' chipped in Brian exuberantly. 'Any time you want a date, missus, I'm your boy!'

'He's a cheeky one, isn't he?' chuckled Ada indulgently. 'Eee, I'm walking on air, with all them lovely songs going round in my head! Away you go now, Nellie, your taxi's waiting. And thanks again — you're a right gem, lass!'

'It must be all them love songs getting to me,' grinned Brian as they started down the path. 'But shall I pay the taxi off? Do you fancy walking home?'

Ellen breathed the balmy air deeply, raising her face to the star-studded velvety sky where a mellow half-moon was spilling softest golden light down over the Dow Hills and onto the river.

'I'd love to walk.'

They spoke little, presently turning away from the river and making their way through quiet, empty streets towards the corner shop. It had been a long but very good day and, like Ada, Ellen found herself silently humming songs. Not the big Hollywood numbers from the show, but the old folk tunes and rounds she and the children had sung together.

'Ma and Jeanette must be in bed,' she murmured as they went indoors. The kitchen light had been left on for them, but everywhere was silent. 'Do you want tea?'

He shook his head, draping his jacket over the chair back and sitting at the table.

'Nor me. I'll go straight up then.' she said. 'I told Jeanette to lie in tomorrow, so I'll be getting up early to do the papers on my own.'

'Give me a knock in the morning and I'll give you a hand.' He watched her as she made for the doorway. 'Nellie! Don't go up yet!'

He was on his feet and across the room, standing before her. Close, but not touching. 'Let's get wed.'

Unwavering, she held his gaze. 'Our promise to marry is an old one, Brian . . . If that promise wasn't already made, would you propose to me now?'

His sharp, shocked intake of breath was audible in the stillness. And that moment of hesitation gave her the answer.

'Nellie, I didn't mean — ' he blurted urgently. 'I'm sorry — '

She silenced his protest with a sad shake of her head. 'We've both changed. So much has happened. The future isn't how we thought it would be anymore.'

'I'm really sorry,' he mumbled thickly, lowering his eyes. 'I thought we might still be able to make a go of it, y'know? I didn't want to let you down.'

Their eyes met warily. She hadn't intended mentioning Jeanette, but suddenly the words were spoken and couldn't be taken back. 'Are you in love with Jeanette?'

He started as though she'd slapped him. Then nodded slowly, looking away.

'I'm glad,' she responded simply, as his face jerked around in astonishment. 'Because, although she may not even realise it herself yet, Jen loves you very much!'

He faltered. 'I — I knew she liked me well enough, but as for anything more . . . ' Almost as an afterthought, he met Ellen's eyes squarely. 'There's nowt going on, Nellie. You do know that?'

'Of course I do,' she answered briskly. 'We can control our actions, Brian, but we can't change how we feel.'

'I didn't want to fall for her,' he confided, glad to get it off his chest at long last. 'For months, I fooled myself into denying it. Then I decided to just ignore it. I figured if we'd got married last year like we planned, I'd have *had* to ignore it!'

When Ellen didn't respond, he scraped back a chair and sat heavily at the table, looking up at her. 'I'll move out, obviously. Get some digs.'

'There's no need. We mustn't make a fuss about this,' she returned sensibly. 'I've had a while to think things over; whether you like it or not, you're part of this family now, and there're others to think about besides ourselves. Jeanette must never, ever get the idea she's responsible for our breaking up. She isn't.

'We're not right for each other, Brian, but we must stay friends.'

'We'd stay friends anyhow, Nellie,' he murmured gratefully. 'So what happens next? We just tell people the news and then go on like normal?'

'For Jeanette's sake — and Ma's — we have to. There's nothing else we can do, especially if you and Jeanette are — are to have a chance of happiness together,' she said, suddenly desperately weary. 'Can you think of a better solution?'

'No.' He paused, turning to watch her go from the kitchen and cross the hallway to the staircase. 'You're a very special person, Nellie Butterworth . . . You and me'll always be best mates.'

'I know we will — that's why I'll be waking you up at the crack of dawn to help me do the papers!' she returned lightly. 'Goodnight, Brian.'

Starting upstairs, Ellen hesitated midway, her cold hand gripping the banister. Drawing in a deep breath, she slowly continued to her room, her face wet with silent tears.

# 15

'That's the ironing finished!' sighed Ellen thankfully, stretching up to place the hot iron on a shelf away from the reach of Peggy and Robbie.

'It's good of you, Nellie, but you shouldn't have come all the way up here today,' commented Ada, folding the ironing neatly into the linen basket. 'You'll have enough to do getting ready for your friend's visit. I could've managed this lot.'

'No, you couldn't. Not yet,' she replied mildly. 'Not even with the new super-duper electric iron!'

Ada glowered up at the object as though it were an abomination. 'Pah! Newfangled nonsense! You can't beat a proper flat iron, heated up by the fire, for a good smooth finish when you're pressing clothes.'

'Those flat irons weigh a ton, they're

clumsy, and Dr Irwin has forbidden you to use them ever again,' countered Ellen with a smile. 'That's why Mr Munro issued strict instructions for me to give them away to the rag-and-bone man when he next comes along the river. And it was thoughtful of him to get this modern, lightweight one for you. It makes the ironing so much easier.'

'Hmm. I suppose I shouldn't look a gift horse in the mouth,' huffed Ada, changing the subject. 'How long is your friend staying?'

'Only a couple of days. Hilary's recently given up her job in Liverpool and left the lodgings we shared,' explained Ellen, fetching a jug of freshly-made lemonade from the marble shelf in the cool larder. 'She's moving up to the village near Southport where her husband-to-be's family live, so they can make a start on planning the wedding and getting their new house ready.'

'I'm glad she's found somebody. I mean, I don't know Mrs Armitage well, only from seeing her in the shop when the pair of you have been up here, but she struck me as a good-hearted sort, and far too young to be a widow for the rest of her life. Widowhood's horrible. Horrible. You be sure to wish your friend every happiness from me.'

'I will!' Impulsively, Ellen stooped to give the elderly woman's plump shoulders a quick hug as she set a glass of lemonade down beside her, placing the other two onto a tray with two slices of almond tart. 'I'll take this out to the children, say my goodbyes, and then I'm off — Poor Hilary will be exhausted after travelling all day in this weather. It's been a real scorcher!'

The dust and heat of afternoon was at its most intense when the old friends were reunited at the bus stop and commenced the long walk through the busy streets across town to the shop.

'Welcome home, lass!' greeted Dorothy, rising shakily to her feet when the kitchen door opened. 'It's grand to have you back!'

'My word, look at you!' exclaimed

Hilary in delight, going to Dorothy and taking both her hands. 'It's wonderful to see you looking so well!'

'I'm not up to clog-dancing yet,' she responded, easing back into the wheelchair. 'But at least I can stand on my own two feet now and again!'

'Hilary!' whooped Jeanette, dashing through from the shop and stopping in her tracks to survey their friend. 'Romance certainly agrees with you — you look absolutely radiant!'

'It's sweet of you to say so,' laughed Hilary, touching fingertips to her flushed cheeks. 'But I think I'm just broiled after the bus ride!'

'Congratulations, anyway!' chortled Jeanette, hugging her. 'You dark horse!'

'Yeah, all the best to the pair of you,' grinned Brian, following Jeanette through the curtained doorway to plant a kiss on Hilary's cheek. 'Nick's a lucky bloke!'

'Thank you, Brian. Nick sends his regards,' she replied warily, conscious of the broken engagement between her two friends and a little unsure of what to say. 'Erm, Nell's been telling me about your new business. Nick will be pleased it's all going so well for you. He's recently opened another bakery in Southport, so the coming months will be anxious for him. There's quite a lot of competition along Lord Street.'

'Ah, no worries! It'll be another little goldmine. Nick's a man of enterprise — same as myself!' he declared, raking his hands through his shock of red hair and reaching for his jacket. 'I've got to scoot — there's a long-handled brush and a bucket of whitewash waiting for me!'

'Some folk have all the fun!' quipped Jeanette, turning towards the shop at the jangle of the little brass bell. 'Are you coming up to the school tonight?'

'Actually, I might be a bit late.' He paused at the door, glancing over his shoulder at her. 'But tell Miss Thwaite I'll definitely come and measure the corridors and classrooms she wants painting, and give her the estimate tonight. I'll get it sorted while you're all rehearsing.'

'Eunice can't abide disturbance or distractions during the Players' rehearsals,' warned Jeanette mischievously. 'So you'd better be on tippy-toes!'

'Nobody will even know I'm there, queen. I'm a dead quiet worker. Used to be a cat burglar before I joined the Navy.' He grinned, slinging his jacket over his shoulder. 'Right, I've gone!'

'Will you be in for your tea?' Dorothy called after him.

'I won't, Dot. Worse luck. I'll just have to starve.' Opening the door, he cast a backward glance to them all and waved a hand. 'Great to see you again, Hilary. Tarrah, each!'

The door rattled shut and Brian was gone. Suddenly the kitchen seemed very quiet, with only the muffled voices of Jeanette and the customer drifting in from the shop. Hilary slid a concerned glance towards Ellen, but her back was turned as she stood at the sink filling the kettle.

★ ★ ★

The following day was cooler, gloriously sunny with a refreshing breeze coming down from the hills, and it was Dorothy who suggested Ellen and Hilary make the most of the weather by going out for the day.

They packed a picnic and set off, crossing the river and taking the familiar track up into the Dow Hills. When they paused for a breather, Hilary raised her face to the cloudless azure sky and sighed contentedly.

'I feel far too lazy for a full-blooded hike. Shall we stick to the low paths?'

'A leisurely stroll will suit me perfectly!' responded Ellen, shielding her eyes and letting her gaze wander the canopy of woodland and the ribbon of swift river, dazzling with sunlight, winding below them. 'We ought to have brought our bathing costumes. We could've swum in the pool below the falls.'

'We'll make do with paddling instead,' smiled Hilary, setting forth once more. 'The shallows near the stepping stones might be a good spot, and we can have our picnic on the knurl under the willows . . . I'm so glad we came out, Nell. I'd almost forgotten how lovely it is here!'

They rambled the hillsides, talking of this and that and nothing in particular, listening to the song of blackbird and mistle thrush, the humming of insects, the chatter of ducks, quarrels of coots and distant, ringing call of a woodpecker.

'It seems years since we last went walking,' mused Ellen, when they plunged from brilliant sunshine into the cool green shade of the woods. 'Suppose it is years! It seems a lifetime even since we came to Whinforth for Ma's last birthday. So much has happened since then.'

'It certainly has,' agreed Hilary quietly, lost in her own thoughts for a moment before turning to her friend. 'How are you, Nell? Really, I mean?'

'Really?' she echoed, expelling a breath. 'Really, I'm not quite sure. I just take it a day at a time. What else is there to do?'

'It must be very painful. Having Brian under the same roof. You're not having any opportunity to, well, put the past behind you.'

'I couldn't have married him. That's the truth of it. Regardless of his feelings for Jeanette, and hers for him,' responded Ellen at length. 'But there's no denying their . . . affection . . . has made getting on with my life far more difficult than I ever imagined. Seeing him day in, day out. It is hard. Does — ' She broke off uncomfortably. 'Does that show, Hilary?'

'Not at all,' she answered at once. 'I'm not sure what I was expecting, given the circumstances. Tension, I suppose. Yet when I arrived, everything was ordinary and comfortable. As though nothing had happened.'

'Brian said exactly those same words the night we broke up, when I asked him not to move out. That we'd be going on as if nothing had happened,' she recalled, and just for a split second, the weariness and strain of going on as usual was plainly etched on Ellen's pinched features. 'We had no choice, really. If we didn't make a song and dance about splitting up, neither would anybody else.'

'Least said, soonest mended?' Hilary nodded. 'It certainly seems to have worked. I don't think I'd have been brave enough to see it through, Nell.'

'It's not getting any easier, though!' she exclaimed desperately, lowering her eyes to the dark, leafy earth strewn with pennies of sunlight dappling through the old trees. 'Brian and I weren't right for each other. So why do I feel such a sense of loss when I see him laughing and talking with Jeanette? I'd be too ashamed to admit this to anyone else, but I'm jealous!'

'There's nothing to be ashamed about,' replied Hilary. 'There've been many occasions, especially sitting alone in a theatre or café, when I've envied all the couples their closeness and companionship. When you've become accustomed to sharing your life, it hurts a great deal to no longer have somebody to share with.'

'I'd never thought of it like that,' Ellen managed at last, going on softly, 'I do wish Brian and Jeanette every happiness, you know. Truly I do. I think they make a lovely couple.'

'So do I!' smiled Hilary. 'They seem very well-matched.'

'Yes, they are,' agreed Ellen, raising her face to the summer sky as the riverside trees thinned and the stepping stones came within sight. Having at long last spoken the worrisome thoughts and feelings that had been weighing so very heavily, she suddenly felt the burden lifted and a lightness of spirit seeping within her. She turned to her old friend, a smile lighting her eyes. 'Are we going to paddle?'

Hilary suddenly shrugged off her rucksack and took off at a sprint. 'Race you to the stepping stones!'

Dumping their packs on the hummocky knurl beneath the willows as they went, the friends shed shoes and socks and scrambled down the sloping bank into the swift-flowing river, gasping at the water's icy coldness.

'You haven't spoken much about your and Nick's plans, Hilary,' remarked Ellen, as they dabbled calf-deep, being careful never to venture too far from the bank, for the river deepened quite suddenly towards the middle and became much faster, an undercurrent rushing along towards the weir beyond the drovers' bridge. 'I'd like to hear all about it. I wouldn't want you to feel you can't talk about your wedding just because I'm not having mine!'

'I did feel a little awkward about it,' admitted Hilary with a smile. 'It's going to be a very quiet affair in the village where Nick grew up. Just his family, and you, really. My brother and his wife are coming up from Derbyshire for the day. Alan's giving me away. We're setting a date at the beginning of October, and then spending a fortnight in Scotland. I've never been north of the border, but Nick knows Scotland quite well, and tells me Loch Lomond is especially breathtaking in early autumn.'

'Oh, Hilary — it sounds marvellous!' exclaimed Ellen. 'I'm so very, very happy for you both! I tried matchmaking so often, and yet you quietly got fixed up all by yourself!'

Hilary laughed. 'I'm probably too sensible to be romantic, but I truly do believe love finds you when and where you least expect it!'

'And Haithe, the village you're moving to,' went on Ellen as they paddled along, tracking the arc of sooty-brown swifts against the cloudless sky. 'What's it like? Have Nick's people lived there long?'

'Generations. His father's retired now, but he used to manage the local bank. They're a very . . . settled . . . sort of family. Mavis and Peter — Nick's parents — asked me to stay with them until the wedding, but I didn't want to impose so I've booked a room at The Blue Bell. That's the village pub.'

'Is your cottage in the village itself?'

'Just a few minutes' walk from The Blue Bell,' nodded Hilary, watching a family of ducklings bobbing amongst the reeds fringing the far bank. 'It's a very old cottage and not large, but such a wonderful place to bring up a family! The garden's a wilderness at present, but I'll plant flowers and make a patch for growing our own vegetables. There's already an overgrown little orchard at the bottom. Oh, I can't wait for you to see it, Nell!

'I've been wanting to suggest something since I arrived,' she went on, as they splashed from the water and began drying their feet and legs with their handkerchiefs. 'You'll be coming to Haithe for the wedding, of course, but it'd be lovely if you could come before then for a holiday. Do you think you'll be able to get away?'

Ellen paused, considering. The notion of taking a holiday had come like a bolt from the blue. 'I'll have to ask Ma and Jeanette, obviously, but Ma is getting so much stronger day by day — '

'Miss Ellie! Miss Ellie!'

She spun around as Robbie Munro came racing through the willows, his father and sister emerging a little way behind.

'Have you been paddling?' he asked, skidding to a halt at the water's edge and twisting around to look hopefully back at Alex. 'Father, can we go paddling? Can we?'

'Another day, perhaps. Robbie, hurry back now!'

Ellen glanced up to see Alex Munro standing on the knurl above them, but he was discreetly looking away from the two barefoot women as he spoke.

'Miss Butterworth, I do apologise for disturbing you. Come along, children!'

Reluctantly, Robbie trailed up the bank but turned to say over his shoulder: 'Have you seen the woodpecker? We've been looking out for him, but we haven't seen him.'

It was Hilary who answered, tying her shoelace and starting up the bank after the small boy. 'We haven't seen him either, but we've heard him several times, haven't we, Nell?'

Ellen nodded, following them up towards

the knurl where the rucksacks were propped against a fallen trunk. 'Deep in the woods, though. Near Boosie's Cave.'

Alex gallantly extended a helping hand to first Hilary, and then Ellen, as they clambered onto the tussocky knurl. Standing before him, Ellen suddenly remembered her manners.

'Oh, sorry! Hilary, this is Alex Munro and his children, Peggy and Robbie. They live at Lane End House, where I've been helping Ada recently. Hilary's come over from Lancashire, Mr Munro. She's staying with us for a few days.'

'How do you do, Mrs — Hilary,' he responded formally, gently taking Hilary's hand once more. 'You seem to have brought a spell of splendid summery weather with you — we've been out walking every day recently!'

'And I see you're carrying Nell's little book with you!' exclaimed Hilary, smiling down at Peggy who was clutching the well-worn volume. 'She told me she'd passed it on! Have you spotted many things?'

'Oh, yes! Lots,' replied Peggy seriously, digging into her pocket for a notepad filled with neat pencil sketches. 'I drew some of them, see?'

'These are very good,' admired Ellen, taking a closer look. 'And you've got the rabbit family just right!'

'I had to sit still for ages while I waited for them to come near enough.'

'We still haven't seen the woodpecker, though,' persisted Robbie gloomily, gazing up at Hilary. 'We look for him every day!'

'Let's see if we can spot him on our way home,' announced Alex, putting an arm about his son's shoulders and starting to shepherd him onwards. 'Come along, Peggy. Good afternoon, Miss Butterworth. Hilary — '

'We're just about to have our picnic!' blurted Hilary, waving a hand at the bulging rucksacks. 'Won't you join us?'

'Yes, please do!' urged Ellen, her own face wreathed in smiles as she looked down at the children's eager faces. 'It *is* almost teatime!'

'That's kind of you — '

'We've enough food to feed a scout troop,' put in Ellen, with a mischievous wink to the children. 'If we don't have some help eating it, we'll have to carry it all the way home again. So you see, you'd really be doing us a great favour if you stayed . . . '

'May we, Father?' begged Peggy. '*Please!*'

'If we stay in the woods a bit longer,' declared Robbie stoutly, 'we may see the woodpecker!'

Ellen raised a questioning eyebrow at Alex. His serious face softened into a warm smile.

'We'll be delighted to share your picnic!'

★   ★   ★

Ellen felt an increasing restlessness in the weeks following Hilary's visit to Whinforth.

Letters were whizzing back and forth between the old friends, and in her mind's eye, Ellen pictured Hilary settling into her new life in the Lancashire village with its squat stone cottages, slate-roofed farmhouses and flat fields of wheat, oats, barley, cabbages and potatoes.

Hilary had a lively writing style, and Ellen had come to know well The Blue Bell and Hilary's room there under the eaves, with its crooked ceiling sloping down to uneven floorboards and the window overlooking the green. She knew her way around Pear Tree Cottage, its overgrown gardens and long-neglected orchard, and felt she could recognise Nick's family and some of the village folk who were to be Hilary's neighbours.

It was Friday evening. The Butterworths had shut up shop and had supper. Brian was working late at the weavers' cottages, in a bid to finish speedily so he could get started painting the corridors and classrooms at Victoria Road while school was closed for the holidays. Jeanette was busy doing her hair and getting ready for a meeting of the Whinforth Players. Ma, Ada and Beattie Clough had gone to the pictures together: *Gone With The Wind* was showing again at the Imperial. Ada had suggested Ellen accompany them, but she'd declined. Alex Munro had mentioned a lecture being given at the lending library on the works of the Brontë sisters. Ellen enjoyed their novels and might well have attended, but in truth, she wasn't in the mood for going out, and instead plumped for having the house to herself, envisaging a quiet evening listening to the wireless and replying to Hilary's latest letter.

She was seated at her dressing-table, just thinking and not doing anything at all, when Jeanette popped her head around the open door. She was barefoot and swathed in a candlewick dressing-gown, her golden hair a mass of tight curls.

'Thanks ever so much for lending me your Dinkies.' She padded in, setting the box of metal curlers onto the dressing-table and considering her reflection in the mirror. 'They're just the best! My hair looks grand, and I haven't even combed it out yet!'

'Why don't you keep the Dinkies, Jen?' suggested Ellen, reaching around to fluff up her sister's shock of curls. 'Your hair takes them much better than mine — *Goldilocks!'*

'Dad used to call me that, remember?' laughed Jeanette. 'But I can't take the curlers, Nellie. You've had them since before the War!'

'And how many times have I used them? Hardly ever!' replied Ellen. 'You'll make much better use of them. Please keep them!'

'If you're sure,' she began, a grin spreading over her face as she clutched the box to her chest, 'I won't say no! I can't believe you're willing to part with them, but if ever you want them back, just say so. OK?'

'Done! Oh, there's a new bottle of setting lotion, too. I never got around to opening it.'

Jeanette took the heavy little bottle of bright blue liquid and paused, meeting her sister's gaze in the oval mirror. 'Nellie . . . Brian's asked me to go to a dinner dance at The Feathers . . . '

'Mmm, I know. I wasn't eavesdropping,' she went on hurriedly, turning to smile up into the younger woman's huge blue eyes, 'I just overheard him talking about it. It's being put on by the Guild and should be quite a grand do. You are going, aren't you?'

'I — I'd like to,' faltered Jeanette uneasily. 'It's just . . . Well, it's like a proper date, isn't it?'

'And what's wrong with a proper date?' demanded Ellen, her eyes warm. 'Of course the pair of you must go! I'll even help you put in your Dinkies!'

'Oh, Nellie!' Jeanette's expressive face glowed with absolute happiness and, setting aside the box of curlers, she flung her arms about Ellen's shoulders and hugged her fiercely. 'You're just the best sister anybody ever had!'

\* \* \*

After some of the younger members of the Whinforth Players had called for Jeanette and they'd set off for their meeting, Ellen took her pen and notepaper into the kitchen, made a cup of tea, turned on the wireless, but really didn't make much of her evening at all. The letter to Hilary petered out after the first dozen or so lines, and Ellen just sat listening to the Light Programme without actually hearing a single note of the music played. She was still sitting lost in a jumble of thoughts when the kitchen door opened and Dorothy returned from the pictures.

'Hello, Ma!' She glanced around cheerfully. 'Enjoy the film?'

'It was beautiful! Never get tired of seeing it,' replied Dorothy, putting her hat and handbag onto the dresser. 'Mind, it was far too warm for sitting in a picture-house really, but they'd left the side doors open so it wasn't that bad.'

'Fancy some cocoa?'

She shook her head, easing off her shoes and putting on soft slippers.

'Tea'd be nice, though. Are you writing to Hilary? Remind me to give you that recipe for Cherry Puffs she asked for. I've got it written out ready.'

'She's seeking out all sorts of fruity recipes,' replied Ellen, warming the teapot. 'There's a little orchard at the back of their cottage, full of old apple and pear and cherry trees. And she says damsons, blackberries and all sorts of fruit grows wild amongst the hedgerows.'

'Must be nice to have a garden,' mused Dorothy, settling at the table. 'Your dad always wanted a garden, you know. He would've made a good gardener. He wasn't afraid of hard work, and he had a lot of patience.'

Ellen smiled, pouring the tea. 'Jeanette and me were talking about Dad earlier on. How he used to call her Goldilocks!'

'So he did! I'd forgotten about that!' chuckled Dorothy. 'She used to think he'd made up the fairy tale about the three bears just for her!

'When are you going to Hilary's for

your holiday, Nellie?' she added, nodding towards the unfinished letter on the table.

'I'm not sure.' Ellen hesitated. 'There's no hurry.'

'Of course there is!' retorted Dorothy. 'Summer's slipping by and you want to make the most of the good weather, such as it is. We'll manage fine in the shop, so don't let that hold you back.

'Since you came back to Whinforth, you've done nowt but work. Here, and then up at Lane End House as well. You need a break, lass. It's high time you started thinking about yourself for a change,' she concluded, putting down her cup and moving from the table. 'I'm off to my bed, but if you take my advice, you'd finish writing that letter and tell Hilary when you'll be coming for your holiday!'

Left alone once again in the solitude of the kitchen, Ellen drew a measured breath and picked up her pen.

Thunder and cracks of lightning had accompanied the hymns and sermon that Sunday morning, and now torrents of warm rain, falling straight and heavy as stair-rods, were slithering down the lancet windows and washing away the dust and grit of the recent dry spell.

A fair few hardy parishioners had braved the downpour and made a beeline homewards from the church, while others hovered in the porch eyeing the sky or tarried around the pews and nave in the hope the Summer storm would soon pass.

Dressed in a crisp check skirt and matching blouse, Ellen wasn't dressed for wet weather; nor was she in any haste to leave the soothing quietude of St. Bede's now the congregation was gradually ebbing away. She lingered with her thoughts, admiring the arrangements of flowers, retrieving a hymn book from where it had fallen beside the lectern.

'Miss Butterworth!'

She straightened abruptly, turning to find Alex Munro approaching from the choir stalls, the service's music still in his hands.

'The singing was glorious today, Mr Munro,' she murmured reflectively. 'Especially the last piece. I can't recall when music has touched me so deeply.'

'Thomas Tallis. His music stirs the soul in a way none other does!' concurred Alex passionately, adding with a small smile: 'The choir scarcely does his work justice, but we try our best and sing from the heart!'

'Surely that's all any composer would wish for,' responded Ellen in a low voice, her gaze drifting beyond him to the west door. Peggy and Robbie were waiting patiently there, while Mrs Heggie chatted to the vicar's wife. 'It was very nice hearing the children singing a hymn on their own, too,' she went on, meeting Alex's thoughtful grey eyes. 'Starting a choir especially for youngsters and giving them their own piece to sing every Sunday morning is a marvellous idea.'

'And once a child discovers the — the *joy* — of singing, that wonder stays with him his whole life long!' agreed Alex enthusiastically, falling into step beside her as she started slowly along the aisle. 'Miss Butterworth — Ellen — I don't wish to pry, but Mrs Heggie mentioned you were returning to Lancashire. Is that correct? Are you leaving Whinforth?'

'I am going away for a while,' she explained as they walked, her eyes downcast upon the time-worn memorial slabs beneath their feet. 'It's just a holiday. Staying with my friend, Hilary. She's recently moved to a village in Lancashire, not far inland from Southport.'

'Ah, I see!' he responded, glancing at her sidelong just as Peggy and Robbie spotted Ellen and instantly left Ada's side, scurrying into the aisle.

'Miss Ellie!' Robbie peered up at her, tugging the sleeve of her blouse. 'Are you going to live at the seaside?'

'Mrs Heggie told us you were going somewhere near Southport,' explained Peggy solemnly, gazing at Ellen through her big round glasses. 'We looked up Southport on one of Father's maps. It's a seaside town overlooking the Irish Sea.'

'We've never been to the seaside!' cried Robbie. 'When you come home, will you tell us what it's like?'

'I'll do better than that!' beamed Ellen, her sombre mood suddenly lightening. 'The very first day Hilary and I catch the bus and go into Southport, I'll send you both a picture postcard of the sea-shore.'

'Could you write us a letter too, please?' asked Peggy shyly. 'Nobody has ever written a letter to us before.'

'Then I shall be the first!' declared Ellen, catching hold of the little girl's hand as they emerged from the west door to discover the rain had all but given way to watery sunshine. 'In fact, I promise I'll write often, and tell you all about the village where I'm staying and everything that happens there!'

They started down through the church-yard, and as they reached the sundial and made to part, the Munro family taking the path winding beneath the yews towards the river and Ellen the main one down into the town, Alex paused.

'Ellen . . . after your holiday,' he began hesitantly, his grey eyes dark as he gazed down at her, 'you — you will be coming back to Whinforth?'

'I'll be home in a few weeks,' she answered at length, looking at the old town unfolding below the churchyard away towards the sweep of river, and beyond the rushing waters to the peaks and woodland of the Dow Hills. 'Whether I'll stay here . . . I don't know, Alex.

'I just don't know what I'm going to do.'

# 16

She and Hilary sharing a room again!

It was almost as though the past year hadn't occurred, reflected Ellen, brushing her hair as she stood at the open window of their room at The Blue Bell, gazing across the village green to higgledy-piggledy stone cottages, well-stocked gardens, copses, orchards and fields of ripening barley and oats bounded by hedgerows and ditches.

Back home in Whinforth, she'd felt increasingly adrift. Without place or purpose or the slightest idea what to do next with her life. Since being here, however, that knot of apprehension and anxiety for the future was gradually unravelling and possibilities were beginning to shape in her mind.

On several occasions, she and Hilary had taken a trip out to Southport and spent the day shopping and exploring.

With its wide, tree-lined streets and arcades of elegant shops, grand hotels, fashionable restaurants, exclusive galleries and the imposing Victorian architecture of its civic buildings, banks and commercial and legal premises, Southport was a busy and prosperous county town yet possessed a sedate, almost genteel, charm Ellen found immensely pleasing.

She'd lost no time in choosing seaside picture postcards to send off to Peggy and Robbie, and wrote newsy little letters to the children, too. Telling them the things she saw and did, what Haithe and The Blue Bell looked like, and all about the forthcoming Fruit Gathering, which was the cause of great excitement in the village. On another visit to Southport, when she and Hilary had called in at Nick's new bakery and café for lunch, Ellen had purchased sticks of pink, minty rock with the town's name running all through the middle for the children, aware they'd never tasted or even seen the seaside sweetmeat before.

And then last evening, when she was glancing through Southport's local newspaper, Ellen caught herself browsing the Situations Vacant column.

'Aren't you ready yet?' called Hilary, emerging from the shop with a laden basket across her arm and pausing beneath the window of The Blue Bell to wave up at Ellen. 'I've bought you your very own pair of gauntlets for the weeding!'

'I'm thrilled!' laughed Ellen, tossing aside the hairbrush and slipping on sturdy shoes. 'I'll be right down!'

★　★　★

Pear Tree Cottage was beginning to take shape. A local man had repaired the thatch, the guttering had been made sound and the plumbing brought up to date. The oak-beamed rooms with their square, small-paned windows were gradually filling up with furniture and rugs and the bits and bobs Hilary and Ellen purchased during their forays into town.

This morning, however, the pair were

dressed in their oldest clothes and tackling the waist-high weeds and brambles choking the neglected beds at the front of the cottage.

'It's a shame there isn't time for us to grow anything before the wedding,' commented Hilary as they worked. 'But Mavis is giving us some bedding plants coming into flower so we'll have a nice show of colour when we move in.'

'The window boxes and hanging baskets she brought round yesterday are lovely,' said Ellen, glancing up to the masses of flowers adorning the ledges and doorways.

'I must be careful not to disturb the earth around that pear tree when I'm weeding over there by the gate,' remarked Hilary. 'According to Mavis, carpets of snowdrops pop up there every spring, followed by crocus and daffs.'

Ellen pushed a stray wisp of hair from her moist forehead. She'd met Mavis and Peter Wainwright — Nick's parents — when she'd first arrived in Haithe, and had visited their home on several occasions since. She liked the Wainwrights, and it was clear the elderly couple were very fond of Hilary and regarded her as part of their warm, close-knit family. Ellen was also gladdened by how happily Hilary was settling into village life and organising local activities, particularly the forthcoming Fruit Gathering, which would culminate in a party and dance held in the barn behind the Wainwrights' farmhouse.

'This is a beautiful place,' she said, watching butterflies flitting amongst the brightly-coloured flowers spilling from the boxes and baskets Nick had put up before going to work that morning. 'You're both going to be so very happy here!'

'What about you, Nell?' ventured Hilary. 'I couldn't help noticing you reading the Situations Vacant in last night's paper. Are you thinking of leaving Whinforth?'

'It's hard to explain,' answered Ellen at length, the trowel idle in her hands. 'It wasn't until I moved back to Whinforth last year that I began realising how much I'd missed living there. In spite of the many years I've been away, whenever that ramshackle old bus rattles over the hills and down across the river into the town, it always feels like I'm going home. Home, Hilary! Where my roots are. Where I'd come to believe I truly belonged.'

'And now that feeling has changed?'

'Ma still needs to take care, of course, but she's active and busy again. You saw for yourself, we can't keep her out of the shop!' replied Ellen, adding with a wry smile: 'I'm surplus to requirements now. Have been for a while.'

'It's still your home though, Nell,' prompted Hilary gently. 'Even if you're no longer needed in the shop, you'd soon find a secretarial post in Whinforth.'

'I can't just . . . I need to find *some-where*. Something of my own!' she continued uncomfortably, bending to the tangle of weeds. 'Jeanette and Brian will get married sooner or later, and they'll naturally set up home together above the shop. It's a big house. There's plenty of room. And Jeanette loves the shop even more than Ma does. She has ambitions and plans for the business . . . They'll obviously go on living there.'

'And you couldn't stay? No, I can understand that.'

'I just couldn't. Not after they're married. I'd feel . . . in the way. Like the spinster sister who doesn't have anywhere she really belongs.'

'You're being very harsh on yourself,' reproved Hilary mildly. 'Nobody, least of all Jeanette and Brian, could ever think of you in that way. However, I do appreciate your misgivings! Widows and spinsters have a lot in common when it comes to finding a place in this world.'

Ellen returned her friend's gentle smile, a note of optimism coming into her voice. 'If I'm to be moving from home, getting a job and finding another place to live anyway, I've started thinking a clean break and making a fresh start somewhere new might be best.'

'It sounds as though you've already decided! You will be going back to

Whinforth though, won't you? At least for the time being?'

The question unexpectedly echoed Alex Munro's words that last Sunday in church, and Ellen was shaken by a sudden, confusing shock of awareness. Her voice faltered, and before she could frame a response, Hilary was going on thoughtfully:

'It's hardly a fresh start, I know, but have you thought about approaching Hathersedge's? I'm sure they'd be only too glad to have you back.'

Ellen shook her head decisively. 'Not Hathersedge's, or Liverpool. 'It'd be like taking a step backwards. I like Southport very much, and there seem to be promising career prospects. I can imagine building a future for myself there.'

'It's certainly an attractive town, and there'll be countless opportunities for a woman with your secretarial skills and experience. Hathersedge's will give you excellent references,' went on Hilary. 'If you do choose Southport, it goes without saying you'll be welcome to stay here with Nick and I until you get your bearings.'

'You're a good friend, Hilary!' Swallowing the lump in her throat, she gave her companion a quick hug before going on with a grin: 'But I'll not be a gooseberry! And talking of fruit, is this Fruit Gathering I keep hearing about some sort of ancient village tradition?'

'Yes. Elderly folk recall it as still being hugely important to the village when they were young, second only to the grain harvest. But gradually it died out until the *Waste Not, Want Not* campaign during the War, when labour and food was in such short supply.

'Apparently, there was an abundance of wild fruit being unpicked and left to rot on hedgerows and trees all around Haithe, so Mavis and the other women decided to do something about it. They gathered the whole village together and revived the Fruit Gathering, sharing out everything picked to help folk through the Winter.'

'And now it's an annual event again?'

'Absolutely. Nick tells me it's gone from strength to strength,' concluded Hilary. 'It's one of those special occasions when everybody in the village works together fruit-picking, and rounds off the day with a party and barn dance in the Wainwrights' field.'

'What actually happens to the fruit?' asked Ellen. 'Does it just go for jam?'

Hilary shook her head. 'Mavis will be in the kitchen all day long. As soon as the fruit's picked, she and women all over the village will use some in tarts and cakes for the party, and then make a start bottling, jam-making and canning. Mavis has this canning machine that came over from America during the War. She tells me it's wonderful!'

'I've never even seen a canning machine!' mused Ellen, visions of convoluted metal contraptions springing to mind. 'How does it work?'

'I've no idea, but we'll soon find out! Oh, I'm so glad you'll still be here!' exclaimed Hilary. 'Fruit Gathering is the Saturday before you go home, and

it's going to be such an exciting weekend — a really *special* way to round off
your holiday!'

★   ★   ★

The day was dry and clear with wispy
fleeces of cloud drifting across a brilliant
blue sky. Anybody who wasn't carrying
a basket, trug or sack, and harvesting
berries, late damsons, crab apples and
hard little common pears from hedge-
row and bushes, was distributing the
fruit around the umpteen kitchens where
womenfolk were cracking on with the
baking and preserving as soon as each
batch arrived on their doorstep.

'I'm glad we're donating everything
from this old orchard to the village.'
Hilary paused from blackberrying and
glanced across to where Nick and Peter
were busy apple-picking. 'It was a lovely
idea of Nick's, and a nice way to begin
our life together at Pear Tree Cottage.'

'Peter was saying this orchard is
particularly sheltered from wind and

gets lots of sunshine, so that's why it brings the apples and pears on so early,' remarked Ellen, disentangling herself from the prickly brambles. 'And the old gardeners planned it very carefully, planting varieties that fruit at different times to give as long a season as possible.'

'There's a nice mixture of trees, too. I'm looking forward to the cherries and apricots next year — ' Hilary broke off, waving to a group of children and dogs hovering at the gate. 'Come along in! We've a barrow over there ready to go to the kitchens — and you'll find a box of biscuits too, if you're hungry!'

'Thanks, missus!' shouted the biggest boy, pushing open the gate and leading the way. Helping themselves to a handful of biscuits before taking hold of the shafts, the children manoeuvred the barrow over the coarse grass, accompanied by four barking and prancing black, brown and white dogs. 'We'll bring the barrow back later!'

'Thanks!' called Hilary. 'How's the baking going?'

'Mrs Wainwright's already made heaps of raspberry buns and jellies for the party,' answered one of the girls, pulling up her baggy ankle socks. 'And my mum's baking sponge cakes and damson turnovers!'

'You're making me hungry!' laughed Hilary as the children trundled from the gate. She glanced at Ellen, who was watching them wistfully. 'Nell, are you alright?'

'Just thinking about Peggy and Robbie.' She gave a quick smile. 'I told them about the Fruit Gathering in one of my letters — are my ears going funny, or can I hear music?'

'That's Jethro with his fiddle!' responded Peter Wainwright from somewhere up one of the old trees. 'He and his pals are playing at the party tonight, but old Jethro'll be sat outside The Blue Bell all day giving us music while we work — it's a handy spot for when he gets thirsty!'

After spending the early part of the morning stooping and scrabbling for berries amongst the hedgerows all around the cottage garden and orchard, Ellen was glad to be standing upright apple-picking. She stepped down from the ladder and gently eased the contents of her jute sack into the waiting barrow.

'Visitors for you, Nell! I've already kitted them out with sunhats and baskets!'

Ellen twisted around at the sound of Mavis Wainwright's cheery voice; squinting up into the bright sunlight, she gasped in astonishment.

'Alex!'

Breaking away from their father's side, Peggy and Robbie burst through the gate and raced across the orchard, laughing and calling to Ellen as she opened her arms for them. 'What are you doing here? I was just thinking about you earlier on!'

'We wanted to come and join in — ' began Peggy.

' — and see the seaside!' chipped in Robbie.

'Ellen,' began Alex quietly, approaching through the long grass and looking quite different in his shirt-sleeves and faded sunhat, a ragged jute sack slung over his shoulder. 'I hope you don't mind — '

'Welcome to Haithe! How lovely to see you all again!' It was Hilary who stepped forward from the berry-picking, making introductions between the Munros and Wainwrights and glancing from Alex to Ellen, and then to Peggy and Robbie, who were curiously surveying all about them. 'Children, I'm a bit stuck over here with the blackberries. Do you think you could help me reach into the tangled bits of the hedge and gather them?'

Peggy nodded eagerly. 'We've never picked fruit before. That lady with the big hat said we could take some of the berries we pick to her house later and she'll show us how the canning machine works.'

'I'd love to see how it works!' exclaimed Hilary, taking their hands and starting across the garden. 'Do you think she'd let me come too?'

'I expect so,' replied Peggy after a moment's thought. 'She was very nice.

She said the secret of canning fruit is to get the number of times you turn the handle exactly right!'

'She said we mustn't pick all the fruit from the bushes,' put in Robbie, hitching his basket higher onto his arm. 'She said we're to leave some for the birds and wasps and wild animals.'

'She's absolutely right, Robbie,' answered Hilary, leading them to the tangle of brambles drooping with plump, blue-black fruit. 'That's very important to remember.'

The boy craned his neck over his shoulder. 'Isn't Father coming to pick berries too?'

Hilary followed the small boy's gaze to where Alex and Ellen were still standing a little apart, not saying anything or even looking at each other yet. 'Your father's so tall, I think he'd be better helping Nell,' she replied loudly and in Alex's direction. 'Poor Nell's been up and down the ladder for hours, I'm sure she'll be glad of a little rest from all that climbing!'

'Oh, yes! Yes, of course!' nodded Alex with alacrity, suddenly galvanised into action and moving toward Ellen and the ladder. 'Thoughtless of me, I'm sorry. Glad to lend a hand.'

'You've arrived at exactly the right moment,' murmured Ellen, looking up at him with a hesitant smile. 'Even with the ladder, I'd just about reached as many as I could.'

He nodded, drawing a slow breath and meeting her uncertain eyes steadily. 'I hope you don't mind our — my — coming here today, Ellen. It was rather an impulse. I decided to hire a car and drive over to see you.

'It seemed such a wonderful idea . . . ' He faltered, still holding her gaze, searching her upturned face. 'However, this is your holiday, isn't it? I realise now, my following you here, just turning up like this, it's really the most dreadful imposition and quite — '

'Alex, enough!' she whispered, her eyes soft. 'I can't tell you how pleased I am to see you!'

'Since our conversation in church — '

'Shirking over by the apple tree!' chuckled Mavis Wainwright, appearing at the gate again, this time with an enormous jug and tray of cups. 'Here's some iced lemonade for the workers — come along, children! Help yourselves, this'll keep you going. As for the apple-pickers — ' She beamed as she passed Ellen and Alex on her way out. ' — I'll need those apples picking if we're to have apple and blackberry tarts for the party tonight!'

★   ★   ★

In the coolness of early evening, with the fruit gathered in and the bottling, jam-making and canning underway, everyone was congregating around the barn in the Wainwrights' field. The sun was sinking low in the west, the sky aglow with streamers of gold, rose madder, scarlet and fiery orange. The flickering night-lights in their heavy glass jars were just starting to come into their own as shadows deepened, and folk began helping themselves to the freshly-baked fare heaped upon trestle tables, and from the barrels of ale and cider and pitchers of lemonade provided for youngsters and abstainers.

There would be music and dancing later, and Jethro and his fiddle had been joined by three other elderly gents with flute, penny whistle and squeeze-box. Ellen and Alex were sitting with their plates and mugs on the hay bales ranging along the barn's open side, watching dusk meld into the velvety darkness of a Summer's night.

It had been a glorious day, reflected Ellen with a contented sigh. A quite perfect day!

' . . . the children get terribly excited whenever they receive your letters, and they were longing to join in gathering the fruit. I'm so very pleased we came today, Ellen. It's been wonderful,' Alex was saying quietly. 'I've booked into The Blue Bell for tonight, and in the morning we'll set off for a day at the seaside

— ah, here they come!'

'My word!' exclaimed Ellen, her eyes shining as Peggy and Robbie bounded into the barn, each clutching a jar with a bright label and frilled floral pot cover. Mavis and Peter Wainwright, and Hilary and Nick, were bringing up the rear, laden with fresh supplies of pies, cakes, pasties, tarts and crusty baps to replenish the tables. 'Whatever have you got there?'

'This is the blackberry jam we helped to make!' cried Peggy, her eyes wide behind their glasses. 'The jars are still warm — *feel!*'

'We turned the handle on the canning machine, too!' said Robbie, carefully propping his jar of blackberry jam onto the hay bale. 'Mrs Wainwright's going to give us our cans tomorrow before we go to the seaside.'

'After we canned the damsons,' explained Peggy, 'we had to put the cans into boiling water for a very long time to heat the fruit right though. Mrs Wainwright said they should be done in time for us to take away with us.'

'Are you coming with us to the seaside?' yawned Robbie, kneading his eye with his fist. 'We're going to build sandcastles tomorrow.'

'Right now, I think the pair of you should be going to bed!' smiled Alex, rising from the hay bale. 'We've an early start in the morning.'

'Why don't you and Nell stay and finish your cider?' suggested Hilary brightly, unobtrusively elbowing Nick in the ribs. 'The dancing will begin shortly, too.'

'Do you know *The Fiddler's Waltz?*' put in Nick helpfully, indicating the corner where the musicians were tuning up on a stack of bales. 'It's Jethro's solo piece. The old codger always starts off the dance with *The Fiddler's Waltz*. It's a beautiful old tune, it'd be a shame if you didn't stay to hear it.'

'We'll take Peggy and Robbie over to The Blue Bell and get them settled,' went on Hilary. 'I've even got a jolly good bedtime story to tell them.'

'Thank you, it's very thoughtful,' began Alex. 'But I couldn't — '

'Course you could! And you'd be doing us a favour, because this is good practice for us!' laughed Nick, crouching on all fours so Robbie might clamber onto his back. 'Would the young gentleman like a pony-ride to the inn?'

The boy didn't need asking twice, and when he was securely seated, Nick led the way from the barn, with Hilary at his side holding Peggy's hand and carrying the precious jars of blackberry jam.

'What a very nice couple,' remarked Alex, glancing over his shoulder at them. 'They're so happy together.'

'Yes,' agreed Ellen softly. 'Yes, they are.'

'Ellen, the children were keen to come here today, but I was too,' began Alex awkwardly, turning to her with a sudden imperative to speak out lest the moment pass and perhaps be lost forever. 'I'm not adept at putting my emotions into words, but since you

341

went away I've been so dreadfully lonely and miserable.

'I haven't been able to stop thinking about everything you said that last Sunday at church. I was afraid you might decide to stay here in Lancashire after all. That I'd never see you again, and you'd never know how very much — '

He broke off, distracted by jovial folk suddenly milling all about them, setting aside mugs and plates and taking partners for the dance. Alex turned to Ellen once more, catching her hands within his own and meeting her eyes urgently.

'Ellen, I wondered — hoped — that perhaps you'd come to the seaside with us tomorrow, and afterwards . . . afterwards, if we mightn't all go home together?'

'Over the hills and home together — I'd like that, Alex,' murmured Ellen, smiling up into his earnest grey eyes and moving into his arms as the first haunting notes of *The Fiddler's Waltz* drifted on the fragrant night air.

'I'd like that very much!'

We do hope that you have enjoyed reading this large print book.

Did you know that all of our titles are available for purchase?

We publish a wide range of high quality large print books including:
**Romances, Mysteries, Classics**
**General Fiction**
**Non Fiction and Westerns**

Special interest titles available in large print are:
**The Little Oxford Dictionary**
**Music Book, Song Book**
**Hymn Book, Service Book**

Also available from us courtesy of Oxford University Press:
**Young Readers' Dictionary**
**(large print edition)**
**Young Readers' Thesaurus**
**(large print edition)**

For further information or a free brochure, please contact us at:
**Ulverscroft Large Print Books Ltd.,**
**The Green, Bradgate Road, Anstey,**
**Leicester, LE7 7FU, England.**
**Tel:** (00 44) 0116 236 4325
**Fax:** (00 44) 0116 234 0205

## WHISPERS ON THE PLAINS

### Noelene Jenkinson

Widowed wheat farmer Dusty Nash, of Sunday Plains pastoral station, is captivated by the spirited redhead who arrives in the district. Irish teacher Meghan Dorney has left her floundering engagement for a six-month posting to the outback of Western Australia. Thrown together in the small, isolated community, each resists their budding attraction to resolve personal issues and tragedy. But when Dusty learns the truth about the newcomer, can he forgive enough to love?

# SUZI LEARNS TO LOVE AGAIN

## Patricia Keyson

Upon meeting troublesome pupil Tom's father, Cameron, young schoolteacher Suzi feels an immediate attraction. She is determined not to be drawn into a relationship, knowing she would feel unfaithful to her late husband; but the more time Cameron and Suzi spend together, the more they are captivated by each other. Suzi rediscovers deep emotions, though she agrees with Cameron that Tom must come first . . . But how long can Suzi hide her love for Cameron?

# THE DUKE & THE VICAR'S DAUGHTER

## Fenella J. Miller

The Duke of Edbury decides he must marry an heiress if he is to save his estates. So far he has managed to stay out of the clutches of the predatory mothers who spend the Season searching for suitable husbands for their daughters. The god-daughter of his aunt, Lady Patience, might be a suitable candidate, and he is persuaded to act as a temporary guardian to both her and her cousin, Charity Lawson. When Charity and Patience exchange places, the fun begins . . .

MLS 11/15

25 JON
14/3/17

05 NOV 2018

21 Nov 2023

07 Jun 24

15 JUL 2017

04/06/2019

DATE Sun
12/18

Books should be returned or renewed by the last
date above. Renew by phone **03000 41 31 31** or
online *www.kent.gov.uk/libs*

# SPECIAL MESSAGE TO READERS

## THE ULVERSCROFT FOUNDATION
**(registered UK charity number 264873)**

was established in 1972 to provide funds for research, diagnosis and treatment of eye diseases. Examples of major projects funded by the Ulverscroft Foundation are:-

- The Children's Eye Unit at Moorfields Eye Hospital, London
- The Ulverscroft Children's Eye Unit at Great Ormond Street Hospital for Sick Children
- Funding research into eye diseases and treatment at the Department of Ophthalmology, University of Leicester
- The Ulverscroft Vision Research Group, Institute of Child Health
- Twin operating theatres at the Western Ophthalmic Hospital, London
- The Chair of Ophthalmology at the Royal Australian College of Ophthalmologists

You can help further the work of the Foundation by making a donation or leaving a legacy. Every contribution is gratefully received. If you would like to help support the Foundation or require further information, please contact:

**THE ULVERSCROFT FOUNDATION**
**The Green, Bradgate Road, Anstey**
**Leicester LE7 7FU, England**
**Tel: (0116) 236 4325**

**website: www.foundation.ulverscroft.com**